Anything for love . . .

"Now, there's someone who needs a love potion," Jessica said, pointing across the carnival lawn to Peter Burns.

"He's hopeless," Janet commented.

"I'm sure he's looking for Mary," Ellen said. "Lucky for her, she's still at the basketball game."

"Hey, Peter!" Jessica called to him. "Don't you want to try some love potion?" This opportunity was too good to pass up.

"Um, no thanks," Peter said, his ears turning pink.

"Come on, it's great," Jessica said. "Whatever girl you want, she'll be yours within twenty-four hours after drinking just one dose of this special potion." She glanced at Janet and almost started laughing. It was going to take a lot more than a love potion to make Mary Wallace fall for Puppy Love Burns.

SWEET VALLEY TWINS titles, published by Bantam Books. Ask your bookseller for titles you have missed:

SWEET VALLEY TWINS

The Love Potion

Written by
Jamie Suzanne

Created by
FRANCINE PASCAL

BANTAM BOOKS
TORONTO • NEW YORK • LONDON • SYDNEY • AUCKLAND

THE LOVE POTION
A BANTAM BOOK 0 553 40694 9

Originally published in U.S.A. by Bantam Skylark Books

First publication in Great Britain

PRINTING HISTORY
Bantam edition published 1994

Sweet Valley High and Sweet Valley Twins are registered
trademarks of Francine Pascal.

Conceived by Francine Pascal.

Produced by Daniel Weiss Associates, Inc., 33 West
17th Street, New York, NY 10011

Bantam Books are published by Transworld Publishers Ltd.,
61–63 Uxbridge Road, Ealing, London W5 5SA, in
Australia by Transworld Publishers (Australia) Pty. Ltd.,
15–25 Helles Avenue, Moorebank, NSW 2170, and in
New Zealand by Transworld Publishers (N.Z.) Ltd.,
3 William Pickering Drive, Albany, Auckland.

Printed and bound in Great Britain by
Cox & Wyman Ltd., Reading, Berks.

One

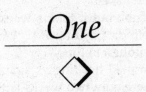

"No, that won't work," Lila Fowler said. "We can't have a booth selling our favorite Unicorn stuff—we don't want *everyone* to think they can be a Unicorn."

"How about a kissing booth?" Ellen Riteman suggested. "You know, one kiss for a dollar."

Jessica Wakefield looked at Ellen as if she had lost her mind. "If *you* want to kiss all the nerds in Sweet Valley, go ahead, but *I'm* not going to do it," Jessica practically exploded. Of all the stupid ideas! A kissing booth at the annual charity carnival? She'd rather be in a pie-eating contest than humiliate herself by kissing someone like Winston Egbert or Peter Burns in public. Just imagining it made her shudder with disgust.

Ellen crossed her arms and leaned back against

the couch in the Wakefields' living room. "Well, at least I thought of something."

"I know—how about a booth selling special paper? The kind we made last week in art class," Kimberly Haver asked.

"That was cool, but it took a week just to make one piece," Belinda Layton said. "We wouldn't be able to finish enough in time."

Jessica drummed her fingers against her empty glass. There were only two weeks left until the carnival, and her club, the Unicorns, had to have the best booth. There was no question about that—the Unicorns were the prettiest and most popular girls at Sweet Valley Middle School. They always made a point of standing out.

Every year, Sweet Valley Middle School held a carnival to raise money for local charities, and the sixth grade was always in charge of the festivities. Finally it was Jessica's turn to get involved, and she couldn't wait.

She heard the kitchen door open, and a few seconds later her twin sister, Elizabeth, walked into the room. "Hey, Elizabeth," Jessica said. "Where were you?"

"I had a *Sixers* meeting," Elizabeth said.

"You had a meeting at school? On a Friday afternoon?" Janet Howell looked appalled. Janet was Lila's cousin, and an eighth-grader. She was also president of the Unicorn Club, which made her just about the most important person in the middle school.

"We were planning the special edition for the carnival," Elizabeth explained.

Lila covered her mouth and pretended to yawn. "How thrilling."

Elizabeth frowned at her. "Actually, Lila, it *is* pretty thrilling. Maybe not as thrilling as talking about hair spray and Mega Mousse . . ."

Jessica stifled a laugh. Watching Elizabeth stand up to Lila was always fun. Her sister thought Lila was silly and snobby, and Lila thought Elizabeth was incredibly boring.

Of course, Jessica reflected, it wasn't surprising that she and Elizabeth had different friends—they were completely different people, even though they *looked* identical. Both girls had long, sun-streaked blond hair, blue-green eyes, and dimples in their left cheeks.

But Jessica spent most of her time hanging out with the Unicorns, or practicing cheers with the booster squad at school. As far as she was concerned, school was for socializing—and maybe a little studying now and then.

Elizabeth, on the other hand, was serious about school. She actually *enjoyed* her classes, and spent a lot of her free time working on *The Sweet Valley Sixers*, the sixth-grade newspaper, and reading mystery novels. It wasn't that she was a book-worm, though—she did know how to have fun. It was just that sometimes Elizabeth had to be *re-minded* to have fun. And Jessica was always happy to remind her. Even though they hung out with different crowds, Jessica still considered Elizabeth her best friend in the whole world.

"I interviewed Mr. Clark today, and he said he's going to hold a contest to see whose booth can raise the most money," Elizabeth said. Mr. Clark was the principal of their school.

"Cool!" Jessica said happily. "I wonder what the winners—"

"Mary!" Tamara Chase exclaimed, as Mary Wallace, the only member of the Unicorns absent from the meeting, barged into the living room with a frantic look on her face.

"Where have you been?" Janet demanded.

"Are you OK?" Mandy Miller asked.

"You're . . . not . . . going . . . to"—Mary paused to catch her breath—"believe this."

"What?" every girl in the room demanded at once.

Mary took another deep breath. "Johnny Buck is coming to Sweet Valley!"

"*What?*" Jessica cried.

"No way!" Mandy shouted.

Mary nodded. "I just heard it on the car radio on the way from the dentist's office. My mom dropped me off at the corner because she was in a hurry to get back to work, and I ran the whole way here. I couldn't wait to tell you guys. Can you believe it?"

"I can't," Lila said. "Why would Johnny Buck play here? He usually plays only in big cities. There isn't even a stadium in Sweet Valley big enough for him to play in."

"That's just it," Mary said. "The deejay said Johnny wants to play some smaller shows on this tour. He's going to be at the Hippodrome."

"But it has only two thousand seats!" Janet protested.

"How are we supposed to get tickets?" Ellen asked. "They'll sell out in ten seconds."

"They won't be for sale. The deejay said there's going to be some kind of contest to win tickets," Mary explained. "He said the details will be in the *Sweet Valley Tribune* on Monday."

"I wonder what we're going to have to do," Jessica said.

"I don't care if we have to stand on our heads for three days straight—I'm going to that concert!" Mary declared.

Jessica grinned. Mary was the only person Jessica knew who liked Johnny Buck more than she did. "You know what, Mary? I'm going with you," Jessica said.

To see Johnny Buck, Jessica would even kiss Winston Egbert. Well . . . maybe.

*   *   *

Saturday afternoon the Unicorns met at the Valley Mall to put up posters advertising the charity carnival.

"I wish we knew what we were advertising," Janet said as she took a neon-pink poster from the stack in Mary's hands and stapled it to the bulletin board just inside the front entrance.

"It doesn't matter. All we have to do is get people to come, and they'll make it to our booth," Mary said. "It's all for a good cause, anyway." She glanced at the window of Kendall's, one of her favorite clothing stores. She wanted a new outfit to wear to the Johnny Buck concert, and she had only two and a half weeks to find one.

"I still can't believe Johnny Buck's going to be right here in Sweet Valley," she said to Jessica as they walked along the east wing of the mall.

"Neither can I," said Jessica.

"Does Elizabeth want to go too?" Mary asked. She was one of the few people who were good friends with both of the Wakefield twins.

"I think so," Jessica said. "I know Amy does, so they'll probably go together."

Mary stopped to put up a poster on the kiosk by the fountain in the center of the mall. She had just finished stapling when she felt someone standing behind her. She turned around and almost bumped right into Peter Burns.

"Hi, Mary," Peter said, smiling nervously at her.

His short brown hair was combed neatly, and he wore a red T-shirt and jeans.

"Hi, Peter," Mary said. She smiled at him, then turned to join the rest of the girls, who were heading toward the food court.

"What are you guys doing?" Peter asked, walking after her.

"Advertising the carnival," Mary said.

"Oh. Right," Peter said, blushing. "I guess I knew that."

Mary shrugged. She never knew what to say around Peter. He always seemed to want to talk to her, but then he never *said* anything.

"Mary, come on!" Janet called to her.

"Listen, I have to go—I'm holding everyone up," Mary said, indicating the stack of colorful posters she was carrying. "Have a good weekend." She smiled at him again.

"Thanks!" Peter said. "You too. I mean, have a good weekend. Maybe I'll see you later." He gave Mary a hopeful look.

"Maybe," she said. "Bye!"

When she caught up to the others outside the music store, they were all staring at her expectantly.

"So, did he ask you to marry him?" Janet asked.

Everyone burst out laughing.

"I've never seen anyone with such a bad crush," Belinda said. "He practically faints every time he sees you."

"His face turned bright red," Jessica added. "Did you notice it?"

"What a geek," Kimberly said with a laugh.

"I don't know why you even bother to talk to him," Lila said. "Or why he thinks he actually has a chance with you. I mean, you *are* a Unicorn, after all. How can he even think it's possible? He might as well go after *me*."

Mary shrugged. The truth was, she didn't think Peter was so terrible. He was cute, in his own way—he just happened to be kind of a nerd, too. It didn't help his image with the Unicorns that he had won second place in the science fair earlier that year. "Well, I don't know what to do. I mean, it's not like I encourage him."

"Maybe you just haven't been rude enough to him," Janet said knowingly.

"Listen to Janet. She's an expert on this," Jessica said with a laugh.

Janet shot her a withering glance. "Very funny, Jessica. Seriously, Mary, when boys you don't like start following you around, you've got to ignore them completely. If they say hi to you, just pretend they're not there. Then, if they still talk to you, tell them to get lost. And if *that* doesn't work—"

"You hire a bodyguard!" Tamara said, laughing.

"I once left a note in a kid's locker because he wouldn't leave me alone," Belinda said.

"What did you say in the note?" asked Mary.

" 'If you don't leave me alone, I'm going to beat you up.' " Belinda shrugged. "It was in fourth grade; what can I say?"

Mary laughed. "I don't want to be too cruel. I mean, he's a nice guy."

"Here's what you do," Jessica said. "Start wearing really ugly clothes to school. Like, mix plaids and stripes, and don't comb your hair—he'll stop liking you, trust me."

Mary hit Jessica playfully on the arm. "Thanks a lot!"

"Maybe you could get Mr. Clark to make an announcement over the PA system Monday morning," Mandy suggested. "Attention, Peter Burns: Will you please come down to the office and get a clue."

Everyone burst out laughing all over again—even Mary. She really was going to have to find a way to let Peter know she wasn't interested in him. She didn't want to be mean, but if he kept hanging around and embarrassing her in front of her friends, she wasn't going to have a choice.

"I hate Sundays," Jessica announced as she walked into the kitchen late Sunday morning.

"*You* hate Sundays. What about me?" Steven, the twins' fourteen-year-old brother, demanded, shoving a dirty dustrag in Jessica's face.

"Get that thing away from me!" Jessica cried, coughing.

"I'm turning into a human dustball," Steven complained. He blew his nose into a tissue. "All because Mom and Dad decided to make Sunday the day of torture."

Elizabeth laughed. "Dusting a few tables isn't exactly torture. Besides, they did make us a great brunch."

"Then *you* do it," Steven said, trying to hand her the dustrag.

"Steven, I think the dust is leaking into your brain," Elizabeth said wryly.

Jessica walked over to the refrigerator to check that day's list of chores. "What?" she exclaimed. "I'm supposed to mop the kitchen floor?"

"I feel better now," Steven said. Grinning wickedly, he shook the rag so that the dust fell to the floor. "Hey, did you shrimps hear about the Johnny Buck concert? Not that you'll be able to go or anything, but—"

"Why won't we be able to go?" Elizabeth asked.

"For one thing, it's on a school night. You know you'd never be allowed to go out," Steven said smugly.

"And you would? Right," Jessica said. "In case you forgot, we're the ones who get good grades around here." She noticed Elizabeth staring at her with one eyebrow raised. "Well, Elizabeth does, anyway."

"OK, maybe so," Steven admitted, opening the

refrigerator and staring inside. "But there are going to be only two thousand tickets to this thing. And I know *I'm* going to get one before you do."

"How do you figure that?" Elizabeth asked.

"I just will, that's all," Steven said. "I don't care what I have to do. Cathy loves Johnny Buck."

Cathy Connors was Steven's girlfriend—they'd been dating for a while, which in Jessica's opinion was a miracle. She didn't understand how anyone could put up with her brother for so long. And Cathy was actually a nice, funny person—and pretty, too. It just didn't make sense.

"Well, I'm going too," Jessica said. "If two thousand people get to go, I'm going to be one of them, no matter what."

"Want to bet?" Steven asked, pouring himself a glass of orange juice.

"Sure," Jessica said. She grabbed a broom from the utility closet in the hallway and started to sweep the kitchen floor. "What should we bet?"

"That depends. Elizabeth, are you in on this?" Steven asked.

"Well . . . OK," Elizabeth said. She took some paper towels and a bottle of window cleaner from the cabinet under the sink. "What's the bet?"

"Whoever doesn't get to see Johnny Buck has to do the winner's Sunday chores for a month," Steven said.

"A *month*?" Jessica repeated, the broom poised in midair.

"That's a lot of torture, Steven," Elizabeth said.

"No, it's not, because I'm going to win," Steven said. "Even if I have to sleep on the sidewalk outside the Hippodrome for a whole week to get tickets!"

Jessica looked at Elizabeth and smiled. "That sounds good, doesn't it? Steven gone for a whole week?"

"Definitely," Elizabeth said. "We might not even mind if you *do* win."

"Don't worry—I'll be sure to bring you guys a couple of concert T-shirts," Steven said.

"Oh, I'm not worried," Jessica said. "I'm looking forward to seeing you clean this house from top to bottom."

"It'll never happen," Steven declared, heading for the stairs. "Hey, Jessica." He pointed to a speck of lint on the floor. "Missed a spot."

Jessica barely resisted the urge to throw the broom at him. She'd show Steven. She couldn't wait to tell him all about the concert—after she'd gone, and he'd stayed home. She was going to go. That was all there was to it.

Two

◇

Monday morning, Jessica was dreaming that she had just won the lottery when she heard a loud pounding on her bedroom door. "Jessica, get up!"

She groaned and rolled over. Everyone was always yelling at her to get up, especially on Mondays.

"Jessica!" Elizabeth came into the room and shook the bed. "You'd better get up or you're going to lose that bet."

"What?" Jessica sat bolt upright and threw the covers off. "What's going on?"

Elizabeth laughed. "Today's the day the announcement about the concert is in the paper."

"But I set my alarm extra early—what happened?" Jessica yawned.

"You probably slept through it, just like you always do," Elizabeth said. "Anyway, here's the deal—the *Tribune* is going to do a random drawing to give away tickets. You need to get a copy of today's paper, clip the entry form, and send it in. They'll draw a thousand winning entries next week, and each winner gets two tickets," she explained.

"But that means—wait a second. I need that paper!" Jessica said, throwing on a pair of jeans and a sweater.

"Too late," Elizabeth said.

"Steven took it?" Jessica picked up two random socks from her messy floor and shoved her feet into a pair of sneakers.

"No, Steven went down to Al's Newsstand to buy as many copies as he could," Elizabeth said. "If you hurry, you can probably catch up to him on your bike."

"What about our copy of the paper?" Jessica ran a brush through her hair and grabbed a purple scrunchy from her bureau. Normally she spent a lot more time on her appearance, but this morning she'd just have to live with a ponytail and mismatched socks.

"You know that saying about the early bird catching the worm, right?" Elizabeth smiled.

Jessica couldn't believe it. Of all the times for her sister to get competitive, she had to choose now? "Then I'd better get to Al's," she grumbled, picking up some quarters and dimes—even pennies—that were scattered on the floor and stuffing them into her pockets. She needed as much money as she could get.

Ten minutes later, she pulled up in front of Al's on her bicycle. Without bothering to lock it, she leaned it against the store and ran inside.

Steven was standing at the counter with a fistful of crumpled one-dollar bills. There was a huge bundle of newspapers next to his feet.

"Thirty papers at thirty cents each—that's nine dollars," the woman behind the counter told him.

"Well, hello, Jessica," Steven said in a phony nice voice as he gave the salesclerk his money. "What are you doing here?"

"Do you have any copies of the *Tribune* left?" Jessica asked, still breathing hard from riding at top speed.

"Let me see . . . here are six," the woman said. "That's all I've got."

"I'll take them all," Jessica declared. She dumped fistfuls of change onto the counter. It took her a few minutes to count out a dollar eighty— half of it was in nickels and pennies—but she had just enough. She wrapped up the newspapers and slipped a rubber band around them to hold the copies together.

Steven picked up his stack of newspapers, and they walked out of the store. "Six, huh?" Steven said.

Jessica gave him a dirty look. "I can still win. It's a random drawing, you know."

"I know," Steven said, hoisting the newspapers onto his right shoulder. "It's just that I'll have twenty-four more entries for them to *randomly* pick out. Who knows? I might even win *four* tickets."

"In your dreams," Jessica said. Suddenly she remembered her dream about winning the lottery. She and Elizabeth had had some psychic experiences not too long ago—maybe the dream was a premonition. Maybe it meant she was destined to win the contest. Maybe if she concentrated really hard, she could will the *Tribune* to pick her entry.

"Now, let me think. If I did win four tickets, who would I give the extra pair to . . ." Steven mused. "I can't really think of anyone. Maybe I'll give them to Cathy's little sister."

Jessica glared at Steven and took off on her bike, leaving him behind. If Steven won the contest and she didn't . . . well, there was really only one solution. She'd have to kill him and take the tickets. He left her no other choice.

"*How* many did you send in?" Ellen asked Mary that day at lunch. The Unicorns were sitting at their favorite table in the lunchroom, which they called the Unicorner.

"Seventy-five," Mary said. "I would have sent

more, but every store I went to was sold out of the *Tribune*."

"Yeah, because everyone's entering this contest," Betsy Gordon said. "Even my brother."

Jessica groaned. "*My* brother sent in thirty entries."

"So did I," Lila said. "I had Mrs. Pervis go pick them up for me, after my father saw the announcement on his way to the business section."

Jessica groaned even louder.

"How many newspapers did you get, Jessica?" Mary asked.

"Six," Jessica said in a dejected voice. "My entry forms will probably get stuck at the bottom of the barrel."

"Not necessarily," Tamara said. "If there are thousands of entries, I don't think it'll matter how many we sent in. It's all going to be a matter of incredibly good luck, anyway."

"I just hope I'm one of the lucky ones when they do the drawing on Friday," Mary said, crossing her fingers under the table.

Mandy leaned forward across the table. "Speaking of luck, Mary, your favorite person just sat down behind you."

"And he's staring at you right now," Lila added. "Have you been ignoring him?"

Mary shook her head. "I haven't even seen him since Saturday."

"Well, you'd better do something," Janet said. "Or else he's going to follow you around forever."

Mary nodded. It was easy for Janet to say that—she wasn't the one who had to be mean. Then again, being mean seemed to come naturally to Janet. Besides, she was really popular, and boys were always falling for her. It wasn't the same for Mary. Since dating Peter Jeffries, she hadn't gone out with anyone.

But Janet was right—she did have to get rid of Peter Burns, and the sooner the better.

"This is going to be more work than I thought," Elizabeth muttered to herself as she picked up another brochure. She was sitting at her desk in the *Sweet Valley Sixers* office later that afternoon, looking through the stack of brochures from all the charities that the carnival would benefit. There was a summer camp for children who couldn't afford it, a center that donated and cooked food for elderly people, and a free art studio that gave lessons to anyone who wanted them. She and the rest of the *Sixers* staff were planning to write articles about each charity. There was a knock at the office door. "Come in!" she called.

"Hi," Peter Burns said shyly, stepping into the office.

"Hi, Peter. What's up?" Elizabeth asked.

"Well . . . I, uh, heard about the edition you're

doing for the carnival," Peter said. "I was wondering if you needed some help."

Elizabeth smiled. "We can always use help around here. What do you think you'd like to do?"

"I don't know. What do you need?" Peter asked, looking around the office.

"Let me think for a second." Elizabeth tapped her pen against the desk. "I know—you're pretty good on the computer, aren't you?"

Peter shrugged. "I guess so."

"Since this is a special edition, we want to make the design a little different. Do you feel like working on that?" Elizabeth asked.

"Sure," Peter said eagerly.

"OK. Why don't you experiment with the computer program," Elizabeth said. "I can show you how it works, if you have any questions."

Peter sat down and immediately started punching keys. "I've used this before—it's fun," he said.

Elizabeth watched Peter try out a couple of different formats, then went back to her reading.

"Uh, Elizabeth, doesn't Mary Wallace work on the *Sixers*?" Peter asked a few minutes later.

"Sometimes," Elizabeth said. "She's a really good typist."

"Do you think she's going to be working here this week?" Peter asked.

"I'm not sure," Elizabeth said. "She might be busy with the Unicorns' booth for the carnival. Why?"

"Oh." Peter shrugged, and Elizabeth saw his neck and face turn pink. "Nothing. I just wondered, that's all." He managed a faint smile.

Elizabeth nodded. *She* wondered whether Mary knew that Peter had a serious crush on her—serious enough for him to start working on the *Sixers*.

Mary left school later than usual on Monday afternoon. She was taking Spanish I, and she'd had to spend extra time in the language lab, practicing for her upcoming oral test.

She was surprised she'd been able to focus on school at all that day, since every other thought she had was about the Johnny Buck concert. No, make that *every* thought.

She could just picture Johnny on the Hippodrome stage, and herself in the front row, looking up at him as he sang. Maybe he'd notice her—the Hippodrome was small enough. And maybe she'd get the chance to meet him, or get his autograph.

She was just about to cross the street in front of school when she heard someone calling her name. "Mary! Wait up!"

She turned around and saw Peter Burns running after her, waving his arms. She had to admit that he was a little goofy-looking, even if he was sort of cute, too. She knew that if Janet was around, she'd tell Mary to keep walking and ignore him. But instead Mary waited for Peter to catch up to her.

He smiled and wiped his forehead, pretending to be exhausted. "Phew. You're tough to keep up with."

Mary laughed. "Where are you going?"

"I'm going over to a friend's house, and I think he lives near you. I thought maybe we could walk together."

"Sure," Mary said as they crossed the street. She wondered how he knew where she lived. *Don't forget—you still have to let him know you're not interested*, she reminded herself. But it wasn't as if he'd asked her out or anything—he was just being friendly. "So, why did you stay after school today?" she asked.

"I'm helping on the *Sixers*," Peter said. "I wanted to do something for the carnival. I mean, the science club is working on a booth too, but I wanted to do more."

"That's nice," Mary said. "I wish I could spend more time helping with the carnival. I'm so excited about the concert, I can't concentrate on anything else."

"What concert?"

"Johnny Buck—you heard about it, right?" Mary asked. If he hadn't, then he really was a nerd.

"Oh, sure," Peter said. "So you like his music, huh?"

Mary nodded. "I'm probably one of his biggest fans. I spent my whole allowance to buy newspapers so I could get as many entry forms as possible."

"You're kidding," Peter said. "You must like him a lot."

"It'll be worth it if I get to go," Mary said. "The only problem is, everyone I know entered the contest. There'll be thousands and thousands of entries to draw from."

"You have as much of a chance as anyone," Peter said earnestly. "Just remember that. And if you sent in a lot of entries, you're probably better off than a lot of people—mathematically speaking, that is." He smiled and blushed a little.

Mary snuck a look at Peter out of the corner of her eye. He really was a nice guy. "Thanks," she said. "Where does your friend live, anyway?"

"Oh, on, uh, Remington Street," Peter said. "I guess I'd better turn here and cut over." He shifted his green backpack from one shoulder to the other. "Good luck with the contest. I really hope you win."

"Thanks," Mary said. "See you tomorrow."

"Right," Peter said. "Bye."

As Mary turned down her street, she thought that she probably shouldn't have been so nice to Peter. It was only going to make his crush worse.

But she liked Peter—not as a potential boy-

friend, but as a friend, at least. He was one of the
few people she'd talked to all day who seemed to
understand how important the concert was to her.

Maybe there was more to Peter than Janet or the
other Unicorns realized.

Three

◇

"I've got it," Jessica said on Wednesday afternoon as she walked up to the pool in Lila's backyard. "I have the ultimate, greatest, best idea ever."

"You're going to give me your extra concert tickets if you win?" Kimberly asked.

"You're going to dye your hair purple?" Lila asked.

"No," Jessica said, frowning at her. Everyone in the Unicorn Club was sitting by Lila's pool, working on the plans for their booth. Jessica was half an hour late, but she had a good reason—she'd gotten ice cream with Aaron Dallas after school. "I know what we can sell at our booth!"

"So? What is it?" Belinda asked.

"Yeah, the suspense is killing me," Janet said with a bored look.

"You know how people always want to know how to make someone fall in love with them?" Jessica said.

"What do you mean?" Kimberly asked.

"Well, you know how people check their horoscopes and get extra superstitious and—" Jessica started.

"You want us to tell people's fortunes?" Mandy asked. "I don't think that would go over very well. Remember what happened when you and Elizabeth thought you could read each other's minds?"

"This is different," Jessica said. "I'm talking about a love potion."

Ellen looked at her suspiciously. "Like in that dumb story we read for English class?"

"It wasn't *dumb*," Jessica said. She looked around at the skeptical faces of the other Unicorns. "See, in the story, this guy mixes up a special drink for a girl he likes. She drinks it and ends up falling in love with this other guy, and, well—you don't need to know the whole story. The point is that this love potion really worked."

"It doesn't sound like it worked," Lila commented. She took a sip of iced tea. "It sounds like it bombed."

"Yeah, she fell for the wrong guy," Janet said.

"Look, I'm not saying we're going to sell a love potion that necessarily works," Jessica said. "But it's kind of a romantic idea, and the people who drink it might *think* it works. It would be fun to watch what happens."

"A love potion," Mandy said thoughtfully. "What would we make it out of?"

"Whatever we want," Jessica said. "But we should probably make it taste halfway decent."

"Isn't that going to be expensive?" Mary asked.

"It doesn't have to be," Jessica said. "Since it's a potion, they only have to drink a tiny bit. It's not like soda or anything."

"I think it's a good idea," Tamara said, dangling her feet in the pool. "It'll be easy to make, and we'll probably sell a lot. It'll be funny to see who buys it."

"And on top of that, it will be good for our image," Kimberly said with a giggle.

"You mean like we have the power to make everyone fall in love with us?" Janet said. "True."

"Yeah, especially Mary," Lila teased. "Well, one person's in love with her, anyway."

"I think we should try it," Belinda said. "The Unicorn Love Potion—it has a certain ring to it."

"Jessica, I have to admit—this is a good idea," Janet said, smiling. "No one else is going to have anything like this."

"What can I say? I'm a genius," Jessica said.

"OK, genius, now start taking notes," Lila said. "We need to figure out how this is going to work. How many bottles of this potion do we want to make?"

"As many as we can," Mandy said. "You know there's a prize for the booth that raises the most money."

"Besides that, we want to donate as much money as we can to the charities," Mary said.

"Speaking of money," Janet said, "how much do we have in our bank account?"

"Twenty-three dollars, last time I checked," Mary said. She was the treasurer of the Unicorn Club.

"Sounds like we're going to have to sell water instead of potion," Kimberly said.

"Not necessarily," Janet said. "I bet we can figure out how to do it. We'll just have to find some money somewhere."

A while later, Jessica knew that now was the time to put her plan into action. If she really wanted to go to the concert, she would have to be devious—after all, even if she didn't win tickets, she could still win the bet with Steven. Lila had sent in thirty entries, and Mary seventy-five—they had better chances of winning than Jessica. And if they did win, they'd have an extra ticket to give to *some*body. Why not her?

"Lila, I bet you have a good idea for how to raise the money," Jessica said, strolling over to Lila's lounge chair. After finishing official Unicorn business, they had all gone for a swim and were now lounging on the Fowlers' sun deck.

"Me?" Lila pulled her sunglasses down on her nose and looked up at Jessica suspiciously. "Forget it, Jessica. Just because I'm rich doesn't mean I have to pay—"

"No—I didn't mean you should pay for everything," Jessica said quickly. She smiled. "It's just that you're so brilliant when it comes to finances."

Lila slid her sunglasses back onto her nose. "True. Well, maybe I could ask my father to help. Maybe he could contribute money for something."

"See? I told you guys Lila was brilliant," Jessica said. She pointed to Lila's empty glass. "Would you like some more iced tea?"

"Sure," Lila said.

Jessica picked up her glass and turned to Mary. "How about you, Mary? Thirsty?"

"Well—sure, I guess," Mary said. "Thanks."

Jessica was starting to walk away when Ellen said, "I'd love some too."

"So would I," Janet said. "And could you bring out some chips, too?"

Jessica frowned as she walked across the Fowlers' patio toward the house. She felt like a waitress!

"Oh, and see if there are any of those peanut-butter cookies left, would you?" Lila called to her.

"Sure thing!" Jessica replied cheerfully. *This better be worth it*, she thought as she walked into the house.

*   *   *

"You're not going to tell anyone, are you?" Jessica asked Elizabeth. They were sitting in Elizabeth's room later that night, doing their homework.

Elizabeth laughed. "No, of course not. I don't want to ruin anyone's illusions that this stuff actually works."

"Who knows? It *might* work," Jessica said. "We might end up making something magical."

"Sure," Elizabeth said. "And the *Sixers* might win the Pulitzer Prize for excellent reporting."

Suddenly Steven burst into the room, smiling in a sinister way. "Guess who I just talked to," he said.

"I don't know. The President?" Jessica asked.

"Randy Knight," Steven said. "He has a job delivering the *Sweet Valley Tribune*. He told me that they've gotten close to twenty-five thousand entries for the Johnny Buck concert drawing—and that's only today. They could get more tomorrow."

Jessica couldn't speak for a second. The depressing news sunk in slowly. "Twenty-five thousand? Are you sure?"

Steven nodded.

"Wow," Elizabeth said. "There's no way I'll win—I only sent in one entry. Maybe Amy will. She sent in about fifteen."

"I doubt it," Steven said. "In fact, I can just picture your and Jess's entries, down at the bottom of a huge bin, being crushed by all the other envelopes—like mine, for instance."

Jessica glared at him. "You don't know—ours could be on the top."

"Nope. Your seven little entries are at the bottom," Steven insisted.

"Well, if they are," Jessica said, "at least they're on top of yours."

"How do you figure *that*?" Steven scoffed.

"You mailed yours first. I had to wait to get stamps from Mom," Jessica said. She shook her head. "Too bad, Steven. Not only is Cathy going to dump you when you don't win tickets, but you're going to be spending every Sunday indoors—"

"Pulling dust bunnies out from under Jessica's bed," Elizabeth finished.

"We'll just see about that," Steven said. "By the way, I hope you guys like the smell of floor cleaner." He laughed and left the room.

"Elizabeth, there's no way I'm missing that concert," Jessica said when he was gone. "Even if I don't win tickets, I'm going to find a way."

"If you do, maybe you could slip Johnny Buck some love potion," Elizabeth said.

Mary pushed her macaroni and cheese around on her plate. She couldn't eat. She wasn't hungry. All she could think about was the concert. There were only twenty-four hours until the big drawing.

All her friends were chattering about the love potion and how much fun it was going to be to dress
up in exotic costumes for the carnival. Mary wasn't
even excited about it—she was too worried about
the contest. She knew she was being silly, but she
couldn't help it.

Lila, who was sitting next to Mary, nudged her
with an elbow. "Check out your boyfriend." She
gestured to a few tables over from them.

Mary glanced up and saw Peter staring at her.
As soon as their eyes met, he looked down at his
tray.

"He's been staring at you for the last ten minutes," Ellen said. "I've heard of bad crushes before,
but this is getting ridiculous."

"Haven't you been rude to him, like we
planned?" Janet asked.

Mary shrugged. "Pretty much," she said, even
though she hadn't.

"Hey, do you guys want to look at the book of folk-
lore I was telling you about?" Mandy asked. "It's got
lots of cool info about witches and potions and spells
and stuff. Maybe it has a recipe for a love potion."

"It'll probably tell us we need gross stuff like
bats' wings and fish eyes," Ellen said.

"Oh, thanks a lot, Ellen." Lila put down the
brownie she'd been eating.

"Well, that's what they always use in the
movies," Ellen said.

"We don't want to poison anyone," Belinda said. "But let's go look at that book—it might give us some good ideas, anyway." She laughed. "I'm always up for a fish eye now and then."

Mary stood up and carried her tray over to the dishwashers' window. She was walking back to join her friends when Peter suddenly stepped in front of her.

"Hi," he said. "This is for you." Peter held out a glossy music magazine with Johnny Buck's picture on the cover. Before he could give it to Mary, the magazine slipped from his hand and fell to the floor. Peter quickly picked it up, brushed it off, and handed it to her. "Sorry about that." His face had turned bright pink.

"I've never seen this one before," Mary said. "An exclusive interview with Johnny Buck. Wow— where did you get it?"

"Oh, my uncle works there—at *Rock It*, I mean. He always brings me new copies of the magazine as soon as they come out." Peter shrugged.

"Are you sure you don't want to keep this?" Mary asked.

Peter nodded. "You'll probably enjoy it a lot more than I would." He smiled at her.

Mary couldn't help thinking he had a really nice smile. She smiled back. She couldn't remember the last time someone had done something so thoughtful for her. She was about to thank Peter when she felt a tug on her sleeve.

"Come *on*, Mary," Janet said. "We have work to do."

Before Mary could say anything, Janet pulled her out of the lunchroom into the hallway where the other Unicorns were waiting. "Did you see how red his face got when he dropped that magazine?" Ellen said, laughing.

"We're going to have to call him 'Puppy Love' Burns from now on," Tamara added disdainfully.

Jessica was giggling too. "What did he give you, anyway? A copy of *Love Stories*?"

Mary held up the magazine. "It was pretty nice, you have to admit."

"Hey, that's a great picture," Jessica said, moving closer to take a look.

"Where did he get that?" Tamara asked. "That's next month's issue." She flipped through the magazine. "Awesome pictures!"

Janet shook her head. "It doesn't matter how good it is—you shouldn't have let him give it to you. Now he's really going to think you like him."

Mary didn't say anything.

"He's definitely head over heels for you," Lila said. "If you ask me, it's time for you to do something more drastic."

"Like what?" Mary asked.

"Start dating someone else—and fast," Lila said.

"Lila's right," Janet said. "It's the only way to

get rid of him. Didn't you used to kind of like . . ."

"Tim Davis?" Mary said.

"That's perfect!" Jessica said. "Tim's cute, he's popular—and he's coordinated, too."

Mary had liked Tim for a long time, but she'd decided to give up her crush when he didn't seem interested in her. He was in eighth grade, and he was one of the best players on the boys' basketball team. He usually hung out only with the really popular crowd—most of them boys. "He's kind of a show-off," Mary said. "I don't know if he'd go out with me."

"Why wouldn't he? You're pretty, and you're a Unicorn," Janet said. "I'll drop some hints to him that you're interested, and all you have to do is start talking to him. Then—presto. You'll get Tim and get rid of the lovesick puppy."

"And if that doesn't work," Jessica said as they headed down the hall toward the library, "we can always brew up an anti-love potion."

Four

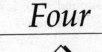

"Did you see this?" Jessica demanded, holding the newspaper in front of Elizabeth's face on Friday morning before school. "They've already drawn the winning entries!"

Elizabeth nodded, swallowing a bite of toast. "I know. But we have to wait a whole day to see if we won." The *Sweet Valley Tribune* had printed a full-page announcement that the winners would receive their tickets by special messengers on Saturday. "Maybe not," Jessica said. She jumped up from the breakfast table and grabbed the phone. "They give a phone number at the bottom of the page."

"They're not going to tell you anything," Steven said, shaking his head.

"This contest seems kind of cruel," Mr. Wakefield commented, pouring himself another cup of coffee.

"Let's talk about something else," Mrs. Wakefield suggested. "If I hear one more word about this contest I think I'll start throwing things."

Mr. Wakefield laughed. "So, how are plans for the carnival coming?" he asked.

"Great," Elizabeth said. "We've done a lot of work on the *Sixers*, and I've heard of some really good ideas for other booths. And the soccer and basketball teams are playing exhibition games."

"Have the Unicorns come up with a theme yet?" Mrs. Wakefield asked Jessica, who had been put on hold at the newspaper.

"Yeah, they're going to paint their faces purple and go as grapes," Steven said. He laughed as he spread jam on a piece of toast.

Jessica stuck out her tongue at him just as someone answered the phone at the newspaper. "*Tribune*, can I help you?" a woman asked.

"I'm calling about the Johnny Buck concert giveaway," Jessica said. "I was wondering if you could tell me if—"

"The winners will be notified tomorrow by three P.M.," the woman said. "Thank you for calling." The next thing Jessica heard was a click, and then the dial tone.

"Pretty rude," Jessica said. "She didn't even wait to hear my question."

"I don't know why you want to find out so badly," Steven said. "I mean, I don't even work at the newspaper and *I* already know you didn't win."

"You can't be sure, Steven," Mrs. Wakefield said. "People who play only one ticket in the lottery often end up winning."

"Excellent point, Mom." Jessica smiled calmly at Steven. "So there."

"Well, don't be so sure," Steven said. "Remember what Randy said—twenty-five thousand entries, and you're only six of those."

"It's true—the odds are against you," Mr. Wakefield said.

"Dad!" Jessica cried. "Don't say that. Think positive."

"You can think all you want," Steven said. "But the winners have already been drawn."

"How's the design going?" Elizabeth asked Peter when she walked into the *Sixers* office on Friday. She was surprised to see him there, since most people didn't stay after school on Fridays. "Pretty well," Peter said, turning from the computer. "Mr. Bowman and I worked on it yesterday and came up with some new things."

"That's great," Elizabeth said. "Can I see?"

"Sure." Peter called up the document on the computer.

"Wow! It's fantastic—the articles jump right out

at you," Elizabeth said. "What's this one—'Buck Concert Causes Riot'?"

"Oh." Peter laughed. "We were just using phony titles, you know, so we could see what it would look like."

"Are you crazy about Johnny Buck too?" Elizabeth asked. "Everyone around here is going nuts, especially Amy. She can't talk about anything else. I even made a bet with my brother and sister about who would win tickets!"

"I did send in an entry," Peter admitted. "But if I won, I probably wouldn't go."

Elizabeth gave him a confused look. "What would you do with the tickets, then?"

"I know someone who's crazy about Johnny Buck," he said. "I'd give her the tickets."

"Who's that?" asked Elizabeth. "Anyone I know?"

Peter cleared his throat. "Well, kind of. Actually, yes."

"Is it Mary Wallace?" Elizabeth asked.

Peter blushed, then nodded. "How did you know?"

"I just had a feeling, from something you said the other day. And she told me about the magazine you gave her," Elizabeth said.

"Did she like it?" Peter asked.

Elizabeth nodded. "Yeah, she thought it was great."

"Do you think—if I did win that contest—would she go with me?" Peter asked.

"She might," Elizabeth said. "I mean, I'm not sure, but she probably would."

"You really think so?" Peter asked eagerly. "Lately I get the feeling that she doesn't like me too much."

"Well . . ." Elizabeth wasn't sure how Mary felt about Peter. "I know she thinks you're a nice person."

"Really?" Peter smiled. "Are you sure?"

Elizabeth shrugged. "As far as I know. Listen, I've got to run. I just came by to pick up some of these brochures. Don't work too late, OK? We still have a week to get everything ready."

"Actually, I was playing a computer game when you came in," Peter said. "I just wanted to hang out here in case Mary came by."

Boy, he really does have a big crush on her, Elizabeth thought. "I think she went shopping with Jessica," she said.

"Oh." Peter shut off the computer and stood up. "Well, I guess I'll take off too."

"Have a good weekend," Elizabeth said as she left. "Good luck in the contest!"

"You, too," Peter said. "You won't, um, tell Mary that I was talking about her, will you?"

Elizabeth shook her head. She didn't want to get any more involved than she already was. She had a feeling that if Mary didn't like Peter, she might have already said too much.

"I love this place," Lila said. "They have so

much cool stuff from the fifties and sixties."

"I know," Jessica said, stopping to look at a rack of sequined blouses. The Unicorns had gathered at the Steamer Trunk, Sweet Valley's best vintage-clothing store. Besides selling antique clothes, the store also rented costumes for special occasions. "Remember when we got the skirts here for the sock hop last year?"

"Those were great," Ellen said. "Even if I did look like an idiot in mine."

Jessica laughed, remembering Ellen's pink skirt with the white poodle embroidered on it. She was glad she hadn't picked out that one.

"May I help you girls?" A saleswoman wearing an old letter sweater, baggy jeans, and saddle shoes walked over to them.

"Yes, please," Janet said. "We're looking for something to wear for the middle-school carnival next weekend."

"Anything particular, or are you just hunting for ideas?" the woman asked.

"Well, we're in a club, and we're selling an exotic love potion," Janet told her. "We want it to seem authentic."

The saleswoman raised her eyebrows. "A love potion?"

"Yeah, isn't it a fantastic idea?" Jessica said. "We're going to sell little bottles of it to everyone who wants to fall in love."

"That is a good idea for a carnival booth," the woman agreed. "After all, the point is to have fun and raise money. And everyone wants someone to fall in love with them."

"Well, *almost* everyone," Mandy said, nudging Mary in the ribs.

"So, what should we wear?" Lila asked.

"Let me think for a second." The saleswoman tapped her finger against her chin. "Hmm. Something exotic . . ." She snapped her fingers. "Here. Follow me." The woman led them past racks of clothing to the back of the store, where the costume section was. "What do you think of this?" She pulled a hanger off the rack. On it was draped a filmy, flowing red skirt, covered by a patterned red top.

"Is that a gypsy costume?" Ellen asked.

"No, it's a sweat suit," Lila said, rolling her eyes. "Of course it's a gypsy costume."

The saleswoman rummaged in some drawers behind the counter and pulled out a turban that matched the outfit. "All you need is to put on some makeup, and maybe some big earrings, and you're all set!"

Jessica touched the skirt on the hanger. "It's kind of . . . sheer, isn't it?"

"That's no problem," the saleswoman said. "A lot of gypsies wore satin pants underneath these—I'm sure I have some around here somewhere."

"Won't we look like we weigh two hundred pounds if we wear pants under a skirt?" asked Tamara.

"No, it's all very thin material—here, try them on and see for yourself." The saleswoman held out a complete outfit to Tamara. She went into the changing room.

"What do you think?" Jessica asked Mary while they waited for Tamara to come out and model the outfit.

"I think it's a really good idea," Mary said.

"Oh, me too," Jessica said. "You know, I really admire your taste in clothes. Have I ever told you that before?"

Mary gave her a strange look. "No, I don't think so."

"Well, it's true. You always look terrific." Jessica smiled at Mary, imagining herself and Mary together at the Johnny Buck concert. "Do you want to go to a movie tonight? I was thinking it might help pass the time until the, you know, until tomorrow."

Mary shrugged. "Sure, a movie sounds good. What do you want to see?"

"I don't care. Whatever you want will be fine with me," Jessica said. She smiled again. It wasn't easy, trying to be so agreeable all the time.

Tamara came out of the dressing room wearing a complete gypsy costume. She walked up to the group, then swirled around, as if she were a model on a runway. "What do you think?"

"I love it," Janet said. "We all need to get one!"

"I'm not sure how many I have in stock . . . but I can always get more," the saleswoman said. "Now, how many do you need, and what sizes?"

While she and Janet went over the details, Jessica sidled up to Lila. "I think you're going to look the best of any of us in that costume," she said with a big smile.

"Really?" Lila asked. "Why?"

"Well, with your long dark hair and all, you'll look the most authentic," Jessica said. "And, uh . . . your hair will contrast with the bright colors of the costume. Hey, you know what? You should ask Janet to get you a purple one."

"That's a brilliant idea," Lila said. She marched up to the counter and talked to Janet for a minute, then came back to Jessica.

"So, what are you doing tonight?" Jessica asked. "Do you want to go to a movie?"

"That depends. What do you want to see?" Lila asked.

"Oh, you choose—I don't care," Jessica said, smiling. She and Lila had been best friends for a long time, so she didn't have to lay it on too thick to guarantee that Lila would choose her to go to the concert. Still, she wanted to make sure she covered all her bases, just in case.

"Actually, I was thinking about that new horror

movie," Lila said, examining some of the antique jewelry in one of the display cases. "What's it called—'Sewer Rats from Hell'?"

Jessica made a face. If there was one movie she did *not* want to see, that was it.

"Of course, we could always see something else," Lila said.

"No—no, that sounds great," Jessica chirped, forcing herself to sound excited. "How about the early show?"

Five

$$\Diamond$$

Jessica took another sip of ginger ale and sighed. She'd been sitting at the kitchen table for over two and a half hours. She'd been there when her parents went to the grocery store, and she'd been there when they came home. She'd watched Elizabeth go for a bike ride to Amy's house, and listened to Steven and his friends play basketball in the driveway with his friends. Steven was now back in his room, playing video games, and Jessica still hadn't moved from the kitchen.

She was determined to be there when the messenger came. But the way things were going, she was going to be an old lady before the stupid messenger showed up.

The telephone rang, and Jessica jumped for it. "Hello?"

"Hi, Jess. It's Mary."

This was it! Mary was calling to invite her. All her hard work had paid off! "Mary—did you win?" she asked.

"I haven't heard anything yet," Mary said. "Have you?"

"No. And it's already twelve thirty," Jessica said, her excitement evaporating. "I feel like I'm wasting my whole Saturday!"

"Yeah, I know," Mary said. "I keep telling myself they must have gone to other neighborhoods first."

"Me too," Jessica said. "Have you talked to anyone who won?"

"No. So far everyone's still waiting." Mary sighed. "It's not looking too good."

"Don't give up!" Jessica said. "I'm not going to, and I don't think you should either, because—wait a second! Mary! A truck just pulled up in front of our house! I'll call you back!" Jessica practically threw the phone down onto the receiver. A truck with the words "Pronto Delivery Service" on the side had stopped right in front of the house.

Jessica opened the door and saw a man in a blue uniform walking up the sidewalk. She couldn't believe her eyes. "You must be looking for me!" she called cheerfully, waving at the man.

"Hello there. Is this the Wakefield residence?" the deliveryman asked.

"It sure is," Jessica said, grinning. "Do you have something for me from the *Tribune*?" Behind her back, she crossed the fingers of both hands.

The man glanced at the clipboard he was carrying. "Actually, I have something for Steven Wakefield. Is he home?"

"S-Steven?" Jessica asked. "No, he's, uh, out playing basketball with some friends. But it's OK—I'll give it to him."

The man shook his head. "No, thanks. I have to hand this envelope directly to Steven himself."

"But—I'm his sister," Jessica said, flashing her sweetest smile. "And he said if you came while he was gone that it was OK to, you know, just leave it with me. I'm sure you have a lot of other deliveries to make, anyway, don't you?" She innocently gazed up at the deliveryman.

He didn't even crack a smile. "I need to speak with Steven, if you don't mind."

"Oh, all right. Doesn't anybody trust anyone anymore?" Jessica grumbled as she led the man into the house. "Steven! Steven!" she yelled up the stairs. "Get down here!"

"Why?" Steven yelled back.

"You won!" Jessica cried.

Her brother flew down the stairs in seconds. "What? I *won*?"

"Do you have some identification, please?" the deliveryman asked.

"Sure." Steven took his wallet out of his pocket and pulled out his school I.D. card. "Is this OK?"

"We have a winner," the deliveryman said, handing the envelope to Steven. "Enjoy the show!" He smiled and turned to leave.

"Excuse me," Steven said. "Before you go, can you tell me if you have any other tickets to deliver to this house?"

The deliveryman glanced at his clipboard. "Nope. Doesn't look like it." He headed back down the sidewalk.

"Steven, don't say anything," Jessica ordered. "Not one word."

Steven danced around the living room, holding the tickets up in the air. "Yahoo! Row twenty-four. Not bad, huh? I'll have a pretty good view of Johnny from there."

"You don't have to rub it in," Jessica muttered.

"Sure I do," Steven said. "You'd do the same thing, and you know it."

"No, I wouldn't," Jessica said, trying to sound innocent. "In fact, if I won, I'd probably want to take someone who wanted to go but couldn't. If I won, I'd take you, or Elizabeth."

"Yeah, right." Steven laughed. "I'm sure I'd be the first person you'd ask."

Jessica tried to look offended. "You would!"

"Yeah, and I'd take you over Cathy," Steven

said. "Right." He shoved the tickets into his back pocket and grabbed his jean jacket from the hall closet. "I'm going over to Cathy's house to give her the good news in person. See you later—loser!" He laughed as he went into the garage to get his bike.

Jessica clenched her teeth as she watched him pedal off down the street. Talk about gloating! She was going to have to put up with Steven's obnoxious attitude for an entire month.

Then she remembered—Elizabeth was in on the bet too. Jessica wouldn't have to do *all* the housework, only half. And if she didn't quite have time to do her share . . . well, Elizabeth wouldn't mind helping her.

"Jessica, you won't believe this!" Elizabeth shouted into the phone. "Amy won! She won two tickets, and she's taking me!"

"That's great," Jessica said, sighing heavily into the phone. "Just great."

"We have seats in the seventh row! Isn't that amazing?"

"Amazing."

"What about you? Did you hear yet?" Elizabeth asked.

"No," Jessica said glumly. "But Steven did."

"You're kidding," Elizabeth said. "Steven actually won? I guess there's no justice."

"You can say that again," Jessica mumbled.

What a nightmare. Both her brother *and* her sister were going to see Johnny Buck—and Jessica was going to be left at home, dusting the furniture from now to eternity.

Mary sighed and flipped another page of the magazine Peter had given her. She'd already read the interview with Johnny Buck at least five times, but it didn't matter—she wasn't reading, anyway. Her favorite Johnny Buck song was playing on her CD player, and she was staring out the window at the stars. Johnny Buck, her favorite performer in the whole world, was coming to *her* town—and she wasn't going to be able to see him.

Come on, snap out of it, she told herself. *It's not the end of the world.*

But it felt like the end of the world. She looked over her shoulder at the wall she'd covered with pictures of Johnny Buck. She'd written out some of her favorite lyrics of his in big, colored handwriting and stuck them on the wall too. If only the contest had been how much you knew about Johnny Buck, she definitely would have won. Instead, she'd lost in a random drawing, and now two thousand other people had the chance to see him. They probably didn't even like him as much as she did.

"Mary! Telephone!" her mother called from downstairs.

Mary walked over to the top of the stairs and leaned on the banister. "Who is it? I don't feel like talking to anyone."

"I'm not sure, but it's a boy," Mrs. Wallace said with a shrug. "Do you want to talk to him?"

"I guess," Mary said, wondering who it could be. She picked up the extension in the upstairs hallway. "Hello?"

"Hi, Mary? This is Tim. What's up?"

"Hi, Tim. Not much. Just sitting around," Mary said. So Janet had told Tim Davis about her—Mary was surprised that even Janet could work this fast.

"Cool," Tim said. "What are you up to tonight?"

"Nothing, really." Mary shrugged. "How about you?"

"I'm seeing a movie later with some guys from the team," Tim said. "Then we'll probably grab some burgers and play video games at the arcade."

"Sounds like fun," Mary said. She didn't know what else to say. Talking to Tim was hard, because she didn't really know him that well.

"Yeah. Listen, the reason I'm calling is I wanted to ask you to the picnic next Sunday—you know, the one after the carnival," Tim said. "You want to go with me?"

At the moment, Mary didn't feel like doing anything. But she knew the other Unicorns would kill her if she said no. "Sure," she told Tim. "That would be great."

"OK. Cool," Tim said. "Hey, did anyone you know win tickets to that concert?"

"Only Amy Sutton," Mary said. "It's kind of depressing. I sent in seventy-five entries and she only sent in fifteen."

"I didn't enter. I think Johnny Buck is totally overrated," Tim said.

"Really? I think he's great," Mary said. "He's my favorite musician, actually."

"I think Major Mercy is much better. I got to see them last summer in an outdoor concert in San Francisco when I was visiting my older brother. You wouldn't believe how great they are in concert," Tim said. "They have this incredible light show that takes like an entire day to set up."

"I don't know them all that well," Mary admitted. Major Mercy was a heavy-metal band, and what songs she did know she didn't like at all. They sounded like people screaming. "Anyway, I just can't stop thinking about this concert, how it's going to be right down the road, practically, and I can't go to it."

"Maybe you can buy someone's tickets from them," Tim suggested.

"I spent all my money on contest entries," Mary said. "I'm broke."

"Bummer. Listen, the movie starts in twenty minutes, so I've gotta go. But I'll see you around, OK?" Tim asked. "And don't forget about the picnic on Sunday."

"I won't," Mary promised.

When she got back to her room, she glanced at the open copy of *Rock It* on her desk. She almost felt bad for Peter—the middle school was pretty small, and he'd find out soon that she was going out with Tim. But what could she do? It wasn't her fault that Peter had a hopeless crush on her.

Besides, Tim was really cute, and at least he had the nerve to ask her out.

Six

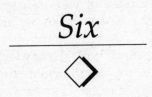

"You all look as if you just found out school's going to last all summer," Mr. Bowman joked at the beginning of English class on Monday morning. "It's not—you can relax."

Nobody said anything. Jessica was tracing black ink circles that had been drawn on the desk by another student. All morning, everyone at school had been moping around—well, everyone except Amy and Elizabeth, and a few other people Jessica didn't know very well. It didn't matter who had won if they weren't going to take *her*.

"OK, today we're going to talk about the story I asked you to read over the weekend," Mr. Bowman said, getting out his notes. "Now, who can tell me what the main theme of the story was?" He looked out at the class. "Anybody?"

No one responded. Jessica heard someone's pencil drop to the floor.

"Is anyone alive out there?" Mr. Bowman asked. "OK. I wasn't going to do this until the end of class, but since none of you are paying attention anyway, I might as well make my announcement now."

"You're canceling class?" Danny Jackson asked.

"Nice try, Danny," Mr. Bowman said, straightening his lobster-pattern tie. "I know you're all upset about losing the Johnny Buck contest. Well, let me tell you—I entered that contest too, hoping I'd win tickets to give to my niece."

"And you didn't win either," Jessica said in a dejected voice. "The odds were one in five thousand. We know, we know."

Mr. Bowman shook his head. "On the contrary. I was sitting at home correcting quizzes when a messenger came to the door. Imagine my surprise when he handed me two tickets to the concert."

"Oh, great," Jessica complained to Elizabeth, who was sitting next to her. "Now even the teachers are rubbing it in that I lost!"

"Now, I could still give those tickets to my niece, Charlotte. But I had a better idea. I've decided to give them—"

"Mr. Bowman, did I ever tell you that English is my favorite subject—and that you're the best teacher I've ever had?" Danny interrupted, a wide grin on his face.

"Thank you so much, Danny. I'm sure you meant every word of that," Mr. Bowman said with a smile. "But no dice. I've decided I'm going to hold a raffle for the tickets," he explained. "It's going to be part of the carnival this weekend. For fifty cents, you can buy another try at the concert—pretty cheap, isn't it? But there's a catch—each person is allowed to buy only one raffle ticket. That way, everyone has an equal chance—and everyone will be able to enter, which means we'll raise even more money for charity. So, how does that sound?"

"Great!" Jessica said.

"That's a really good idea, Mr. Bowman," Ellen said. "Can I buy a raffle ticket now?"

"After class, Ellen," Mr. Bowman said sternly. "Now, do you think we could get back to the story?"

Jessica smiled as she opened her textbook. She wasn't about to give up hope as long as there was any chance of going to the concert. Even though her luck had been rotten lately.

"Isn't it great that Mr. Bowman is raffling off his tickets?" Jessica asked Mary later that afternoon.

The Unicorns were meeting on the front steps of school to go shopping for love-potion ingredients.

Mary nodded. "Only, I bet a couple thousand people will enter the raffle, too."

"Come on—cheer up, you guys," Belinda said. "I can't stand hanging around so many sad people. We still have the carnival to look forward to," she reminded them.

"And it's going to be a blast," Mandy said cheerfully. "Especially with our costumes. We'll have to make sure someone takes our picture on Saturday."

"I'll ask my dad to bring his camera," Kimberly said.

"Uh-oh—nerd alert," Jessica whispered to Mary. Mary looked up at the school entrance and saw Peter headed straight for her. There was no time for her to disappear into the crowd and avoid him.

"Hi, Mary," he said, standing a few steps above her. "Elizabeth told me you didn't win tickets. I'm sorry."

Mary shrugged. "It's OK." Out of the corner of her eye, she saw Janet glaring at her. She tried to act unfriendly, the way Janet would.

Instead of going away, Peter walked down the steps toward her. "You know what? After you told me how much you wanted to go, I even entered that contest. I thought maybe I could win for you." He shrugged. "No such luck."

This time, Mary was the one who blushed. Peter had tried to win for her? While everyone else was being so competitive, he'd thought of her first. But she couldn't let him keep talking to her—Janet was standing right there, listening to every word. "Look, Peter, I—"

"So we didn't win," Peter said, "but I was wondering if, well, maybe you wanted to do something else the night of the concert—like go to a movie or play miniature golf or—well, whatever." Peter looked hopefully into her eyes.

Before Mary could say anything, Tim Davis slid down the railing in the middle of the stairs and landed right at her feet. "Hey, Mary, what's up?"

"N-nothing," Mary said, smiling nervously.

"So, what do you think?" Peter asked. "Do you—"

"Listen, Mary, I talked to my dad yesterday, and he said he could drive us to the picnic on Sunday," Tim went on, completely ignoring Peter. "I told you I'm playing in the exhibition basketball game at the carnival, right? Do you think you'll have time to come watch?"

"Yeah, probably," Mary said. She glanced at Peter. He looked even worse than she had felt when she realized she wouldn't be seeing Johnny Buck.

"See you," Peter mumbled, then he practically ran away from her.

"Hey, I have to go—basketball practice," Tim said. "Catch you later." He sauntered off to join a group of guys on the team.

"That was beautiful," Janet said, smiling at Mary. "I think Tim really likes you!"

"See—I told you my plan would work." Lila grinned.

"Peter will definitely leave you alone from now on," Jessica said. "I think you just broke his heart big-time."

Mary smiled faintly. She wasn't sure which was worse: having Peter like her, or having him hate her, the way he probably did now.

"I wonder where we should start," Tamara said when they got to Findlay's Market.

"The potions aisle?" Jessica suggested.

"That must be in the health and beauty section," Belinda said, laughing.

"Let's just wander around and see what looks good," Janet said.

"Everything looks good—I'm really hungry," Jessica said, staring at a towering display of choco-late-chip cookies.

"I know," Mary said. "I was so upset about the concert, I couldn't eat anything all weekend. Now I'm starving!"

"You know, if I win the raffle, I'm going to take you to the concert," Jessica said. "You deserve to go."

"Really? You'd do that for me?" Mary asked.

"Of course," Jessica said. "You're only the biggest fan Johnny Buck ever had."

"Well, if I win, then I want you to go with me," Mary said. "OK?"

"Deal," Jessica said as they headed down the baking-supplies aisle. "Hey, how about using honey in the love potion?" Jessica asked, holding up a jar.

"That's a good idea," Lila said. "It should taste sort of sweet." She pulled a package of food coloring off the shelf. "Maybe we should make it a color, too."

"And you know *what* color," Janet said, looking at the package. "Red and blue make purple."

"How about some almond flavoring?" Ellen suggested, looking at the rack of spices and flavors.

"I don't think so," Jessica said. "Maybe lemon and honey would be good together, though."

Lila shook her head. "That sounds like a cold remedy, not a love potion."

Jessica frowned at her. "Let's hear your suggestion, then."

"Well, if it's purple, maybe it should taste like grapes," Lila said.

Jessica was about to tell Lila exactly what she thought of her idea when she remembered Lila had a chance of winning the raffle. "We could try it," Jessica said generously.

"How about putting cinnamon or nutmeg in it?" Mandy asked.

"We could—but I have that stuff at my house, so we don't need to buy any," Jessica said. "Actually, we probably have most of this stuff, even the food coloring."

"Your parents won't mind if we use it?" Janet asked.

"No, not at all—and that way, we'll have more money to pay for the costumes," Jessica said. At least she hoped her mother and father wouldn't mind. How could they say no to charity?

"Maybe you should be the treasurer," Mary said, smiling at Jessica.

"Jessica? No way!" Lila said, shaking her head. "She's terrible with money."

Jessica forced herself to smile. "Lila's right—you really can't trust *me*." *Only one more week of this*, she consoled herself. *Then you can be as rotten to Lila as she's being to you!*

"All right, Jessica—where did you put them?" Steven demanded, glaring at Jessica when she got home later that afternoon. He looked absolutely frantic.

"Put what?" Jessica set her backpack down on the living-room couch.

"My tickets to the concert!" Steven barked. "Like you didn't know!"

"I didn't," Jessica said with a shrug. Suddenly she turned to stare at him and her eyebrows shot up. "Are you trying to say . . . you *lost* the tickets?" She burst out laughing.

"I didn't lose them—you *stole* them," Steven said, "and I'm not going to let you get away with it."

"Steven, I didn't take your tickets," Jessica said calmly. "They're probably in your room somewhere."

"No, they're not," Steven said. "They're not anywhere. I've looked all over the place."

"Well, don't panic," Jessica said. "They have to be *some*where."

"Yeah, somewhere like your room," Steven retorted. "Just because you're the only one here who's not going to the concert doesn't give you the right to take my tickets!"

"I didn't!" Jessica protested. "To prove it, I'll help you look for them. But, if I do happen to find them, then you have to take me to the concert instead of Cathy. Or Cathy and I will go, without you."

"No way!" Steven cried. "That's all part of your plan, isn't it? You'll pretend to help me look, and then 'find' them—forget it."

"I don't *have* a plan," Jessica said. "Here, let's look upstairs for them, OK? Don't have a heart attack—we'll find them."

Steven bounded up the stairs with Jessica on his heels. He headed straight for her room. "The first thing I'm going to do is search—" He stopped as he threw open the door. "I couldn't even find a *car* if it was in here."

Jessica's room was never neat, but that afternoon it was especially messy. There were piles of clothing all over the floor, along with magazines, books, and cassettes. It was impossible even to see the floor, except for one small spot by the bed. "You want to search—go ahead," she said.

"You said you'd help," Steven complained. "If you don't, I'll be buried alive in here."

"OK." Jessica started sifting through her clothes. "But this is pointless anyway, because I didn't take your tickets."

"We'll see," Steven said, hunting through the drawers in her bureau. They were practically empty, since all of her clothes seemed to be on the floor at the moment.

Half an hour later, Jessica was sitting on the bed, watching as Steven tried to pry up a corner of the carpet. "If you can't get under there, how do you think I could?" she asked him.

"All right, I give up," Steven said. "The tickets aren't in here." He stood up and brushed off his jeans. "That only means that you've hidden them somewhere else—you were too smart to hide them at home."

"What do you think—I buried them in the backyard like a dog?" Jessica joked.

"Did you?" Steven asked.

"No!"

"Then you must have left them at school—in your locker," Steven said.

"Go ahead and check, if you want," Jessica said with a shrug. "It's number 212, and the combination is 24-13-22."

Steven grabbed a piece of paper from Jessica's desk and wrote down the information. "Tell Mom and Dad I might be late for dinner," he said, before running down the stairs and out the door.

Jessica laughed and shook her head. Steven was losing his mind! She hadn't thought about actually stealing his tickets—but she wished she had. She loved watching him squirm!

Seven

"He's incredibly cute," Jessica said to Mary as they watched Tim play basketball on Wednesday afternoon. "I mean, if I weren't already sort of going out with Aaron, I could like him."

"And he really likes you," Lila told Mary.

"You think so?" Mary asked. "How can you tell?" Tim had asked her to come to his game, but other than that, he hadn't spoken to her very much except for the occasional "hey" when she saw him in the halls.

"I just can," Lila said. "I mean, all Janet had to do was hint that you were interested in him, and he called you right away, right?"

"I guess so," Mary said.

"Then he has to like you," Lila said. "If he didn't, he wouldn't have called. He would have ig-

nored you—the same way you ignored Peter
Burns."

Mary thought about Peter for a second. These
days, he was the one ignoring *her*. When she said
hello to him, he barely replied. She had gotten rid
of him, all right—for good.

"Did you see that shot?" Jessica cried just as the
buzzer went off. "Tim totally faked that guy out."

"He's really good," Mary said, watching Tim
walk off the court. When they stood up to leave, he
hopped over a few bleachers toward them.

"Did you catch that move?" Tim asked them,
wiping his face with a towel.

"It was great," Mary said, smiling. "You played
a really good game."

"I know," Tim said. "Eighteen points and twelve
rebounds. I always count them in my head."

Mary nodded. Even if he was good-looking,
Mary couldn't help thinking that Tim was conceited. It was one thing to know you played a great
game, but it was another to brag about it. "Well,
time to hit the showers," Tim said. "Make sure you
guys come to our game at the carnival, OK?"

Mary nodded. "I'll be there." She had expected
him to say "Thank you for coming," or ask her
what she was up to that afternoon. All he seemed
to care about was whether or not she watched him
play.

"He's cute, but he's a show-off," she commented

to Lila and Jessica as they walked out of the gym.

"Yeah, but he kind of has a right to be," Jessica said. "I mean, he's good."

"And you guys look great together," Lila added. "I think it's so cool that you're a couple. And it's great for the Unicorns' reputation, too."

Mary couldn't believe Lila. It mattered more what Tim looked like than what he acted like? Did that mean they should all go out with good-looking jocks, even if they were jerks? *Yep,* said a little voice in her head, which she decided to ignore.

I'm probably still in a bad mood because of the concert, Mary thought. *I'll give Tim another chance—maybe he just made a bad first impression.* Everyone deserved a chance to prove themselves—even boys.

"Steven, you're not eating anything," Mrs. Wakefield observed that night at dinner. "Are you feeling all right?" Steven was famous for eating seconds, thirds . . . sometimes even fourths.

Steven grunted, pushing his fork back and forth through the mashed potatoes on his dinner plate. "No."

"Is it a cold?" Mr. Wakefield asked, passing a basket of rolls to Jessica. "Do you think you have a fever?"

"Actually, he's suffering from a bad case of amnesia," Jessica said.

"What do you mean?" Mrs. Wakefield asked.

"He can't remember where he put his tickets to the Johnny Buck concert," Elizabeth said.

"I'm sure they're somewhere around the house," Mr. Wakefield said. "Have you looked?"

"About fifteen times," Steven said.

Jessica took a sip of lemonade. "I'll make a deal with you."

Steven frowned at her. "I don't want a deal—I want the tickets."

"I know. And I'm willing to help you find them," Jessica said. "You only have to promise me one thing."

Steven shook his head. "I'm not giving them to you if you find them. You can forget about it."

"Listen—all I'm saying is, *if* I find them, and *if* I have no other way of getting to the concert, then you have to agree to give me one of the tickets," Jessica said. It sounded like a fair bargain to her. "That way, you could still give the ticket to Cathy, only I'd go with her instead of you. You don't even *like* Johnny Buck that much, so it's not like you'd really be missing anything. And Cathy will think you're a great guy for giving up your ticket for me."

Steven didn't say anything for a minute. He took a bite of chicken and chewed it slowly.

"That sounds like a pretty good deal to me," Mrs. Wakefield said. "And who knows—just having Jessica help might lead you to the tickets, and you wouldn't have to give one to her after all."

Jessica frowned at her mother—that wasn't the plan at all. But she noticed Steven's face brighten a little at the thought.

"Yeah, I think that's a fair offer," Elizabeth added. "You'd have to give up only one ticket to get one. It's better than not having any."

"Trust me on that," Jessica said, looking gratefully at Elizabeth.

"OK," Steven said. "But first I want Jessica to swear to everyone here that she didn't take the tickets from me and hide them somewhere, so that she could find them later on and have one."

"Do you still think that?" Jessica asked. "Steven, I'm not that dumb. If I had stolen them, I'd be keeping *both* of them, not turning one over to you."

"Is that so, Jessica?" asked Mr. Wakefield, raising one eyebrow.

"That's not to say that I would ever steal anything from you," Jessica hurried to add. "Because I wouldn't. And I didn't take the tickets." She gave her father an angelic smile.

"I'm glad to hear it," Mr. Wakefield said, nodding. "You sounded like a hardened criminal there for a second."

"We'll start looking after dinner," Jessica said to Steven. "Just for a half hour or so, before we start our homework." She glanced at her father and smiled again.

"You're going to need a vacuum cleaner if you start your search in Steven's room," Mrs. Wakefield said.

"More like earth-moving equipment," Elizabeth joked.

Steven clutched the table. "Do you think—maybe—they got eaten by the vacuum last weekend when we were cleaning?" He jumped out of his chair and started toward the kitchen.

"Steven, don't you dare rip open the vacuum bag!" Mrs. Wakefield ordered. "It's not in there. I'm sure of it. The vacuum hasn't seen the inside of your room in weeks."

Jessica laughed. "Come on, Steven, chill out. If you have a heart attack, you definitely aren't going to that concert."

"The first thing we have to do is retrace your steps," Jessica said. "You've seen them do that on TV, right?"

Steven looked doubtful. "Yeah, so? Who do you think you are—Jessica Wakefield, Private Investigator?"

"Hmm. It does have a certain ring to it," Jessica said, sitting down on Steven's bed. "OK. When's the last time you remember seeing the tickets?"

Steven collapsed into his desk chair and put his

head in his hands. "I don't remember. That's the point."

"Come on, you have to remember something," Jessica said. "Did you bring them to school? Did you put them under your mattress?"

Steven shook his head. "I remember the messenger coming, and then I went over to Cathy's house to show her the tickets—"

"That's the last time I saw them," Jessica said. "You stuck the envelope in your back pocket on your way out the door."

"No, I remember that I had them when I came back from Cathy's," Steven said.

"That's right—you were waving them in my face while I was trying to set the table." Jessica frowned. "I tried to grab them, and you stuck them back into your pocket."

Steven looked at Jessica, an expression of sheer panic on his face. "But—t-those jeans—l-laundry basket—" he stuttered. He jumped up and ran out of the room. Jessica followed him at top speed down one set of stairs, and then another, to the basement.

Steven threw open the lid of the washing machine. Inside, multiple pairs of jeans were swimming in soapy water. Steven shut off the washer and Jessica peered into it. She started pushing the jeans around, digging her hands into the bottom of the washer. She couldn't feel anything. She picked up each pair of jeans and stuck her hands into all the pockets.

"Do you feel anything?" Steven asked eagerly. He was pacing back and forth in front of the washer.

"Wait a second." Jessica pulled a wad of water-logged paper out of one pocket. "I think this—it might be—" She excitedly unfolded it and discovered . . .

The science quiz she had failed last Tuesday. "Oh." For once she was glad her mother had forgotten to check the pockets. "Never mind. That wasn't it."

Steven frowned. "This is hopeless," he muttered.

"Don't give up yet," Jessica said. "You still—*we* still—have six days to find them."

"If I don't find those tickets, I'll never forgive myself," Steven grumbled as they trudged back upstairs.

I won't forgive you, either, Jessica thought.

"We still haven't figured out the recipe," Mandy said as the Unicorns walked into the Steamer Trunk on Thursday afternoon. "Doesn't that make you guys kind of nervous?"

Jessica shrugged. "We have all afternoon tomorrow. How hard can it be to make a love potion?"

"Yeah, it's not like we haven't thought about it," Tamara agreed. "We know it has to be purple, and it has to taste sweet."

"Why don't we just use grape soda?" Ellen suggested.

Lila ignored her. "My father called the place

where we're going to get the little glass bottles. They're ready to be picked up, and he gave me a check for the exact amount. We can get them after school tomorrow on our way to Jessica's house."

"How are we going to carry them on our bikes?" Tamara asked.

"They're really small—if each of us brings an empty knapsack, we'll be able to do it," Lila said. "My father told them to pack the bottles carefully."

"It was really nice of him to help us by donating them," Mary commented as they waited for the saleswoman to finish helping another customer. "And it was great of your mother to give us all those labels, too," she said to Belinda.

"Yeah, if we hadn't had help, we wouldn't have been able to afford to rent these costumes," Janet said. "As it is I had to get an advance on my allowance."

"Who didn't?" Jessica said. "I've had so many advances on my allowance, I probably won't be caught up until I'm sixteen."

"Hello, girls!" the saleswoman said, walking over to them. "I have all your costumes ready—let me get them from the back for you."

"So, have you done anything with Tim lately?" Lila asked while they waited.

"Not really," Mary said.

"What did he say to you when we were walking

out of school today?" Jessica asked.

"Not much. He was talking about basketball again. Something about average points per game," Mary said. "I think that's the only thing he ever talks about, besides Major Mercy—they're his favorite band."

"You don't seem to like him very much," Jessica said.

"No, he's OK," Mary said. She wasn't going to give up on Tim yet. The picnic would be a good chance for them to spend some time together. She just hoped Tim would talk about something other than himself.

"All right, here they are!" The saleswoman came out of the back room carrying a huge box, which she set on the counter. "Take a look."

The girls crowded around the box, pulling out the costumes. "Here's mine," Lila said, grabbing a purple one. She unfolded it and held it up against herself. "What do you think?"

"That looks fantastic," Jessica said. "Mary, let me see yours!"

"I think this is going to be the best booth the carnival has ever seen!" Janet said, examining her own costume.

"You know what? I bet we're going to sell all the love potion we make," Mandy said, fixing a turban on her head.

"I know I'll come by to see you," the saleswoman said. "I could use some love potion myself! Besides, I want to see all these costumes in action. I think I'll take a picture to post in the store."

"Really?" Jessica asked. "That would be so cool. Mary, hold up your costume so I can see how it'll look on you. That green is beautiful!"

Mary grinned. She was suddenly feeling much, much better. Who needed to worry about boys when you had friends like these? The carnival was going to be great!

Eight

◇

"I think we've finally got this right," Elizabeth said, holding up a freshly printed copy of the *Sixers* special edition. "I don't see any more typos, and it looks great. Thanks for all your help, Peter."

Peter just shrugged. "No problem."

Elizabeth gave him a sympathetic look. Ever since Mary had decided to go out with Tim Davis, Peter hadn't been the same. Elizabeth saw him moping around school, and he didn't have half the enthusiasm for working on the newspaper that he had started with. "So, are you excited about the carnival tomorrow?" she asked him.

"A little, I guess," Peter said, sounding very *un-*excited.

"I am," Elizabeth said. "You should see what my sister and her friends are doing. It's—well, I can't tell you, because she swore me to secrecy. But it should be pretty good." She checked on the printer, which was set to print five hundred copies of the four-page paper. Elizabeth had a feeling she was going to be there very late, baby-sitting the printer and making sure the paper feed didn't jam. She needed to have them all ready by nine o'clock Saturday morning. Mr. Bowman had promised to come by at around five to see how things were going. Other than that, Elizabeth was on her own.

"Well, I guess I'll take off," Peter said. "Call me if you need any help, OK?" He picked up his green backpack from the floor.

"Thanks, Peter. I'll see you at the carnival, right?" Elizabeth asked.

Peter nodded. "I'm helping with the big volcano eruption at the science-club booth."

"Is it safe to come check it out?" Elizabeth asked.

Elizabeth was glad to hear Peter laugh. "Yeah. Our orders are to avoid death and destruction," he said.

"Well, come by the *Sixers* booth and visit me," Elizabeth said. "I'll be there almost all day, except that I want to go to Todd's basketball game."

Peter's smile turned into a frown at the mention of basketball. "Yeah, well, I think I'll skip that," he said. "See you later."

Elizabeth wanted to kick herself for mentioning basketball. That had made Peter think of Tim, and then Mary . . .

Elizabeth couldn't help thinking it was a shame that Mary had chosen Tim over Peter. Peter might not have much of a jump shot, but he was an awfully cool guy.

"How about maple syrup?" Jessica was standing on a step stool in front of her kitchen cabinets, listing all the possible love-potion ingredients to the rest of the Unicorns.

"Sounds good to me," Mary said. "It tastes good, and it'll make the potion thicker."

Jessica set the syrup on the counter. "Chocolate syrup? Corn syrup? Olive oil?"

"Eewww," Tamara said, making a face. "That combination sounds disgusting." She, Mandy, and Kimberly were busy writing labels for each bottle. They'd been chosen for the job because they had the nicest handwriting.

Jessica laughed. "Just wanted to see if you were listening. How about some caramel sauce? Butterscotch?"

"Too thick," Lila said. "It wouldn't even come out of the bottle."

"Well, we definitely don't want tomato sauce," Jessica said, pushing some cans aside to see what was behind them. "Or applesauce, or vinegar—"

"I think we should use fruit juice as the base," Mary said. "Then add some things to it, like a tiny bit of syrup to make it thicker, and some spices, maybe."

"Yeah, let's start experimenting," Janet said, "or we'll be here all night."

"OK." Jessica hopped off the step stool and got a bowl out of the cabinet. "We'll start small, until we know what we want to put in. Then we can use a huge bowl." She set the bowl on the table in front of Mary. "Fruit juice first?" Mary nodded.

Jessica poured some cherry-grape juice into the bowl. "Now what?"

"A little syrup," Janet said. "But only a little or it'll be too sweet."

Jessica added some syrup. "Now some spices?" She carried over a selection from the counter.

"Here, I'll do it," Janet said. She picked up three or four jars and shook different powders into the juice. She stirred it with a wooden spoon, then lifted the spoon to her lips. "Mmm . . . this is going to be—disgusting!" she cried, spitting it out in the sink. "That was the vilest thing I have ever tasted." She rinsed her mouth with water and made a horrible face.

Jessica examined the spices Janet had used. "Janet, I think the garlic powder was your first mistake," she said dryly. She dumped what was left in the bowl into the sink and rinsed it out. Behind her, she could hear Lila and Mandy laughing.

"I don't see what's so funny," Janet said, wiping her mouth on a paper towel. "Someone else has to try making the next batch."

"I will," Belinda said. She poured in the juice, then a little more syrup than Janet had. "Let's see . . . what would go with cherry-grape?" She sorted through the cabinet. "I don't know if this'll work, but I'll try." She dumped some lime Jell-O powder into the bowl. "And maybe a little of this . . ." She added half a bottle of vanilla extract and stirred it all together.

A few seconds later, Belinda was spitting out version number two. "Yuck! That was even worse than the time we tried to make banana-cream pie in home ec and forgot the bananas."

"Hey, let me go next," Ellen said. "I have a good idea."

Jessica looked at her and shrugged. It was possible, though not very likely. "Go ahead."

Ellen took some bottles and boxes out of the cupboard.

"This could take a while," Jessica said. "How are the labels coming, Mandy?"

"Great. We've only got—"

"Ellen, what are you *doing*?" Lila cried.

Ellen held a box of baking soda above the bowl full of juice. "This is going to work—trust me," she said.

"That bowl is too full!" Tamara yelped just as Ellen shook some baking soda out of the box. But instead of a few sprinkles, a gigantic clump fell out and splashed into the bowl.

Suddenly the mixture started foaming, higher and higher, until the liquid spewed over the edges and onto the floor, spreading like something out of a scary movie.

"Ellen!" Jessica cried as everyone ran from the creeping concoction.

"What did you put in there?" Janet demanded.

Ellen was pulling paper towels off the rack and throwing them onto the floor. "Just some lemon juice and a little vinegar."

"And half a box of baking soda!" Tamara said, wiping the goop off her shoe.

"I thought a foaming love potion would look good," Ellen said, mopping up the mess. "I can't help it if half the box came out by mistake."

"Does the word 'spoon' mean anything to you?" Kimberly asked.

"We're supposed to be making a love potion. The science club is taking care of the volcano," Janet said critically.

"Yours didn't come out any better," Ellen retorted, shoving the dirty paper towels into the trash.

"Why don't we just look in a cookbook?" Mary suggested calmly.

"We tried that, remember? Love potions aren't in cookbooks," Jessica said.

"No, not under 'love potion'—we'll look under 'punch,'" Mary said. "We can make a fruit punch. You know they always have those recipes for hundreds of people, for parties and stuff. Where are your cookbooks?" she asked Jessica. "We just need a basic one."

Jessica handed her a large cookbook that Mrs. Wakefield used all the time. Mary checked the index in the back, then flipped to the beginning of the book. "Here it is. Fruit Punch, Pineapple Punch, Strawberry-Orange Punch—"

"Let's make the pineapple punch, only color it purple," Jessica said. "I have good luck with pineapple recipes."

"Purple Pineapple Love Potion!" Janet cried. "I love it!"

"Mary, you are a genius," Lila said.

"You know what? I told my dad what we were making and he said purple is the color of passion," Ellen said. "Maybe we should call it Purple Pineapple Passion Potion."

Tamara, Mandy, and Kimberly turned to stare at her. "We just finished writing three hundred and fifty labels," Mandy said. "Do you actually think we're going to start over?"

"So what ingredients do we need?" Lila asked, ignoring Ellen's suggestion.

"Tea, lemon juice, orange juice, sugar, pineapple juice, ginger ale, and soda water," Mary said.

Jessica grinned. "Thanks to Mary, I think we might actually make a potion without exploding our kitchen."

"Thanks to the cookbook, you mean," Mary said. "This potion might even taste good."

"If it would only work, too, then we'd really be onto something!" Mandy joked.

"Watch your feet," Mrs. Wakefield said when Elizabeth came into the kitchen at six o'clock that evening. "I don't know what happened in here, but my feet are sticking to the floor. I'm going to have to get Jessica to mop again."

Elizabeth smiled. "Who knows *what* will be in that potion." She lifted the lid off a pot of spaghetti sauce. "Mmm . . . this smells great. I'm starving."

"We'll eat in a few minutes," Mrs. Wakefield said, "as soon as your father's famous garlic bread is done. Did you get all your copies of the *Sixers* printed?"

Elizabeth nodded. "All five hundred. I know the articles word for word. I'll probably be reciting them in my sleep." She ran upstairs to put her backpack in her room. When she came back down, she found everyone else in the living room. "Hi," she said. "What's going on?"

"Steven and Jessica are arguing about whether he could have left the tickets at Cathy's house," Mr. Wakefield said with a sigh. "They could just call her and ask, but that would be too easy." He smiled at Elizabeth.

"I can't ask her," Steven protested. "She'll think I'm such a loser!" He knitted his eyebrows thoughtfully. "I guess I could search Cathy's room when she's not looking."

"Steven left his brain the same place he left the tickets," Jessica explained helpfully.

"You sound desperate," Elizabeth said.

"I am," Steven said. "The concert's only four days away."

"Why don't you enter the raffle at the carnival tomorrow?" Elizabeth suggested.

"Elizabeth! Did you have to tell him about that?" Jessica complained. "That's one more person to compete against *me* in the drawing."

"I think you're *all* losing your minds over this concert," Mr. Wakefield said, shaking his head.

"Steven, have you really looked everywhere in the house?" Elizabeth asked. "The garage? The bathroom?"

"Yeah, I've looked in every— Wait a second. I never looked in *your* room!" Steven jumped off the couch and ran up the stairs. Jessica was right behind him.

"You guys don't think *I* stole the tickets!" Elizabeth yelled after them.

Mr. Wakefield shook his head and picked up a magazine. "They're going crazy. And they're driving *me* crazy."

Elizabeth ran up to her room. By the time she got there, her room looked more like Jessica's room. Steven and Jessica were crawling under things and throwing clothes around. At first Elizabeth was furious, but her sister and brother looked so ridiculous running around and tearing apart her room that she had to laugh.

"Hey, you guys, I don't have Steven's tickets," she said. "So don't bother looking."

"Maybe I dropped them in here," Steven said. He flung a notebook over his shoulder.

"Hey—watch it!" Elizabeth said, catching the notebook in midair. "Anyway, why would I need to steal anyone's tickets? I'm already going to the concert."

This only made Steven and Jessica search the room more intensely. "I am not losing that bet," Steven grumbled as he crawled under the bed.

"Neither am I," Jessica replied, looking behind the chest of drawers. "No way."

For some reason, probably because they were both being so obnoxious, Elizabeth was really enjoying seeing them squirm. "Yeah, it's going to be a great concert," she said in a loud voice. "I can't wait. Don't worry—I'll tell you guys all about it. . . . Did I mention we're sitting in the seventh row?"

Steven crawled out from under the other side of the bed and flung a pillow at Elizabeth, just as Jessica tossed a stuffed animal at her.

"If I were you I wouldn't make too much of a mess," Elizabeth warned. "You're only going to have to clean it up later!"

Nine

◇

"Are you really going to wear that in public?" Steven asked when Jessica came downstairs on Saturday morning.

Jessica made a face at him. "You don't have to take your bad mood out on me. It's not my fault you can't keep track of two lousy tickets for more than an hour."

"I think you look great," Elizabeth said. "The costume's a little wild, but it'll work really well for selling love potion."

"Mom put on some eye makeup for me," Jessica said. "Does it look OK?"

"Sure, if you don't mind looking like a raccoon," Steven said.

There was a car honk outside, and Elizabeth glanced out the window. "I think your limo is here," she said. "Lila's father's limo, to be precise."

"I'll see you at the carnival!" Jessica said, grabbing her purse and heading out the door.

"Happy Halloween!" Steven called after her.

Brothers, Jessica thought, walking carefully down to the car. She hadn't worn her dressy sandals in a while, and she wasn't used to the heels. The back door of the limo swung open as she approached it. "Here she is, Ms. Love Potion!" Mandy called.

"You guys look fantastic," Jessica said, sliding onto the seat beside Mandy. Both Mary and Lila were in the car, and Mr. Fowler was in front with the driver.

"Daddy came along to help us set up," Lila told Jessica. "I think he was a little nervous about having five hundred breakable bottles in the trunk." She laughed.

"Did you try any of the potion today?" Mary asked Lila, who had stored the bottles of potion overnight.

Lila nodded. "I took a sip, and it was fine. Daddy tried it too—he wanted to make sure we weren't selling anything poisonous."

"Did he like it?" Jessica asked.

"He said it was pretty good, and he's waiting for someone to fall in love with him." Lila laughed.

"Maybe we should each drink a bottle," Mandy said. "It might make life interesting around here."

"Well, speaking of interesting," Jessica said, "Elizabeth told me Mr. Bowman wants her to help him with the raffle drawing after the carnival today. So it looks like I'll know who won before any of you."

"Oh, right, Jessica," Lila said. "As if Elizabeth will tell you anything—she's too honest for that."

"We'll see," Jessica said smugly.

The carnival was being held at Secca Lake, and there were already several cars in the parking lot when they arrived. Mr. Fowler had the chauffeur pull up as close to the park as possible to unload the car.

Mr. Clark was waiting by the main entrance, at a desk marked "Booth Registration." "Good morning," he said to the girls. "The Unicorn Club, I presume?"

Jessica nodded. "Where's our booth?"

"Let me see." Mr. Clark consulted a sheet of paper on the table. "You're in luck—you're close to the food concessions. Everyone's going to pass your booth whether they like it or not. You're booth number twenty-two."

"Yes!" Mandy said happily. "Thank you."

"Do you need any help setting up?" Mr. Clark asked. "There are some parents roaming around who volunteered to help."

"I think we can get everything," Lila said. "I mean, my father and his driver can."

"Then good luck," Mr. Clark said. He cleared his throat. "By the way, would you mind telling me what your booth is all about?"

"We're selling a love potion," Jessica told him. "Only a dollar a bottle, and it's guaranteed to work."

Mr. Clark looked skeptical.

"Well, it's guaranteed to taste good, anyway," Jessica amended. "You'll have to come buy a bottle!"

"And don't wait too long, because it might just sell out!" Mary added.

At one minute before nine o'clock, when the carnival began, the Unicorns were ready. They'd put up their poster and decorated the booth with brightly colored crepe paper. Mary put some sample bottles of the love potion on the booth table, and they'd stored the rest in ice in large plastic buckets behind the counter.

"Love potion? What's that?" asked their first customer, a boy who looked about eight years old.

"If you drink it, it will make someone fall in love with you," Lila told him.

"Gross!" He moved on to the next booth, where the football team was selling football-shaped chocolates wrapped in foil. Across the way, the soccer team was raffling tickets to a professional soccer game in Los Angeles. Jessica caught Aaron's eye and waved to him. Beside his booth, the chess-club booth had a computer chess game people could try to beat for a dollar.

Jessica liked being in the thick of things. As the park began to fill up with people, she got more and more excited. By ten o'clock, there was a crowd in front of their booth.

"Love potion, huh?" a middle-aged man in a baseball cap asked. "Well, it's worth a shot." He gave them a dollar and downed the bottle in one gulp.

"You know, this reminds me of a pineapple punch I once made for a party," an elderly woman commented to Mandy after she took a sip from the bottle.

"How much money do we have?" Jessica asked after a while.

"We've already sold seventy-eight bottles," Mary said as Lila sold another two bottles to a high-school couple. "And it's only ten thirty."

"Excellent," Lila said. "And here comes a definite sale."

"Hey," Tim said, sauntering over to the Unicorns' booth. "What's up?" He was wearing a white T-shirt that said "Make It Count" on the front and "S.V.M.S. Annual Charity Game" on the back.

"We're making lots of money," Mary said. "Do you want to try some love potion?"

Tim picked up one of the sample bottles and examined it. "What's it taste like?"

"Pineapple," Mary said. "It's really good."

"OK. I'll take three," Tim said. He took three dollars out of his pocket and gave them to Mary. When she handed him three bottles, he opened them all at once and drank them down one after another.

"So everyone's going to fall in love with me now?" Tim said. He winked at Mary. "It says right here—guaranteed."

Mary smiled faintly. "I guess it must work, then."

"So you'll be at my game, right? It starts at noon," Tim said.

Mary nodded. "I'll be there."

"Cool. See you." Tim wandered over to the soccer team's booth.

"He is totally in love with you," Jessica declared when he was gone. "He bought three bottles—without even stopping to think about it—and then, *then*, he asks you if it's going to work!"

"I don't know," Mary said. "I think he was only doing that to impress the rest of you."

Mandy shook her head. "The only one he wanted to impress was you. Didn't it work?"

Mary shrugged.

"What?" Lila demanded. "Are you telling me you don't like Tim Davis—after you've had a crush on him for a year? What's not to like? He's cute, and funny, and he's good at sports—"

"I know," Mary said. "It's just—I think he cares

more about himself than anyone else."

Lila flipped her long brown hair over her shoulder. "What's wrong with that?"

"Nothing," Mary said. "I guess I'm just not like that."

"I don't know," Jessica said, staring at Tim as he made his way from booth to booth. "If I were you, I'd be really happy that he liked me. I mean, you could do a lot worse."

Mary didn't say anything. She turned to help a group of kids.

"What's wrong with *her*?" Lila whispered.

Jessica shrugged. "I don't get it. It's almost as if she'd rather be dating Puppy Love Burns!"

"Get your paper here! Hot off the press!" Amy called from her seat at the *Sixers* booth. "Only fifty cents!"

"Amy, you're really good at this," Elizabeth said. "You must have been a paperboy in a former life." She looked at the stack of newspapers on the booth desk. "We've gone through about a hundred already." She glanced at her watch. It was almost one thirty.

"I can't believe how many people are here," Amy said. "I think it's twice as many as last year."

"Maybe it just feels that way because we're involved this time," Elizabeth said.

"Hey, lady, got change for a dollar?" Mr. Wakefield asked, stopping in front of the booth.

"Hi, Dad," Elizabeth said. "I'm glad you came."

"I wouldn't have missed this carnival for anything," Mr. Wakefield said. "Your mom will be by in a minute—she's checking out Jessica and her love potion. Actually, we'll probably stick around here for a while. We had to get out of the house."

"Uh-oh. What's Steven doing now?"

"He's cleaning the entire house, from top to bottom, to find those missing tickets." Mr. Wakefield shook his head. "And leaving a path of destruction behind him."

"Steven—cleaning?" Amy burst out laughing.

"I hope he finds those tickets soon—or we're all going to lose our sanity," Mr. Wakefield commented. "In fact, I'm heading over to Mr. Bowman's raffle booth right now."

"Don't tell me *you* want to go to the Johnny Buck concert," Amy said.

Mr. Wakefield raised one eyebrow. "I wish I'd never heard of Johnny Buck. I want to win tickets for Steven so that life at our house can go back to normal." He shook his head again and walked off into the crowd.

Elizabeth and Amy laughed. "All I can say is, I'm glad our tickets are at your house," Elizabeth said. "Where they're safe!"

A few minutes later, Peter stopped by the booth.

"Do either of you want to take a break?" he asked. "I can fill in for a while."

"Not yet," Elizabeth said. "How about in an hour or so?"

"OK. I'll come back," Peter said.

"How's the science-club booth?" Amy asked.

"The volcano's rumbling right now," he said with a smile. "I'm walking around, checking out other booths. Then I want to buy one of Mr. Bowman's raffle tickets."

Elizabeth gave him a quizzical glance and he shrugged.

"I can always dream, right?" he said quietly, and she knew just what he was talking about.

"Now *there's* someone who needs love potion," Jessica said a little later that afternoon. She pointed at Peter, who was standing at a booth across the way.

"He's hopeless," Janet commented, shaking her head as she made change for another customer. "Did you guys see how much money is in here?" She peered into the cashbox. "How many bottles do we have left?"

"Only a couple, I think," Tamara said. "I'll check." She started rummaging in the ice buckets for bottles.

"Peter's probably looking for Mary," Ellen said. "Lucky for her, she's still at the game."

Peter walked by slowly, looking as if he was

trying to decide whether to stop or not.

Jessica stood up, forgetting her painful feet. This was too good an opportunity to pass up. "Peter, don't you want to try some love potion?" she called to him.

"Um, no thanks," he said, his ears turning pink.

"Come on, it's great," Jessica said. "Look, we practically sold out already. And it works, too. Whatever girl you want, she'll be yours within twenty-four hours after drinking just *one* dose of this special potion."

"I don't think so," Peter said. "I don't really believe in that stuff." But he didn't move on, either—Jessica had a hunch that he was beginning to soften.

"If it doesn't work," Jessica said, "we'll give you your money back. Just find us at school on Monday, and we'll refund it."

"No questions asked," Janet added.

"Wait a minute," Tamara said. "I think we're completely *out*."

"No way," Jessica said. "We sold all five hundred bottles?"

Tamara nodded. "There aren't any here. Even the sample bottles are gone."

"Thanks anyway," Peter said, starting to walk off.

"No—don't go," Jessica said. "I can mix up another batch in about fifteen minutes. Come back then, and I'll give you a fresh bottle. Tell you what—I'll make yours extra-strength."

"Jessica has a special recipe," Janet said. "It's been handed down through her family for generations."

"Yeah. That's how my father met my mother, actually," Jessica said.

"Really?" Peter looked hopeful. "Well, OK. It's for a good cause, even if it doesn't work."

"Oh, it'll work," Jessica said, nodding. "Trust me."

"I'll be back in fifteen minutes," Peter said, walking on to the next booth.

When Jessica turned around, Janet was crouched behind the booth, laughing. "That was brilliant!" she gasped between laughs.

"How are you going to make another batch here?" Tamara asked. "We don't have any of the stuff."

"I'm going to make a special Puppy Love Potion," Jessica said. She grinned. "I don't know what it'll taste like, but I know one thing—it'll never work!"

"I should have taken that last shot, instead of Todd," Tim said as he and Mary walked through the carnival after the game. "He always hogs the ball."

Mary didn't say anything. She didn't know a lot about basketball, but from what she had seen, Tim had been the one who was hogging the ball most of the time.

"Yeah, and the coach shouldn't have taken me out, just because I got a couple of fouls, either." Tim shook his head. "I hate when he does that. It's not fair."

Talk about a sore loser, Mary thought as she and Tim approached the raffle booth. At first she had tried to be sympathetic, but after listening to Tim complain for ten minutes, she was barely even paying attention.

At the booth, she saw Peter buying a raffle ticket from Mr. Bowman, and the two of them were laughing. "Just a second," Mary said to Tim. "I want to ask Mr. Bowman about the raffle."

"I'm going to get something to drink." Tim rubbed his throat. "That stupid potion made me really thirsty."

Mary didn't feel like pointing out that playing basketball for two hours probably had more to do with it than any love potion. She walked up to Peter. She felt as nervous now as he had been the week before.

"Hi, Mr. Bowman. Hi, Peter," she said. "How's the raffle going?"

"I hate to tell you this, because I know how much you like Johnny Buck, but I've sold an amazing number of tickets," Mr. Bowman said. "Add Peter's, and it makes about six hundred."

"Well, it's better than twenty-five thousand," Mary said, shrugging. "Right?" She looked at Peter.

"Yeah," he said. She waited for him to say something else, to comment on the odds, but he didn't. Still, he was buying a raffle chance. Could that mean he still wanted to win for her?

"So, you decided you wanted to go after all?" she asked him.

"Maybe," he said, sounding very relaxed. "But things might turn out OK even if I don't."

"What do you mean?" Mary asked.

"Oh, never mind," Peter said, looking around the carnival.

Mary felt like hitting Peter over the head with her sandal. How could he have gone from being so nice to being so cold in a week? He was acting as if he didn't even want to talk to her. He obviously hadn't liked her *that* much, after all.

"Ready to go?" While Mary had been staring at Peter, Tim had come back, carrying two large cups. "Here, I got you a soda too."

Mary turned away from Peter. "Thanks. That was so nice of you, Tim," she said, smiling sweetly at him.

She turned to see if she was making Peter jealous, but he was gone.

Ten

Jessica picked up one of the many empty potion bottles that their customers had left behind and headed over to the food concessions. She didn't have any money, so she would have to make Peter's special love potion out of whatever she could find that was free.

She stopped at the Mexican food booth and put a spoonful of hot salsa into the bottle. *I'll tell him that it's hot because it's a LOVE potion,* she thought. Then she headed for the booth with hamburgers and hot dogs, and added some yellow mustard to the salsa. She mixed them together, and the potion turned orange. She needed to at least try to make it purple.

Then she glanced at the soda her father had bought her, which she'd been carrying around for the last hour. "Root beer—perfect!" she said under her breath. She poured a little of the leftover soda into the bottle, put the cap on, and shook it. Now the mixture looked sort of gray.

There was a booth sponsored by the Indian restaurant in town, and Jessica stopped there next. She spotted some different sauces in various dishes. She was going to ask the man working at the booth what they were, but he was busy waiting on people.

Well, here goes nothing, Jessica thought, adding a little of each to the potion. She hoped Peter had a strong stomach.

On her way back to the Unicorn booth, with just a few minutes to spare, Jessica stopped at the funnel-cake concession and put some powdered sugar on top of the reddish potion. It looked festive, if not edible.

"What did you put in that?" Janet asked when Jessica returned. "It looks like sweet and sour sauce."

"That's basically what it is," Jessica said. "Well, more like hot and sour." She smiled. "After Peter drinks this, his breath will be so deadly that he'll probably never get a date."

"He'll probably make us give back his money," Tamara said.

"It'll be worth it," Janet said. "In fact, I'll put in the extra dollar myself."

Peter came by a few minutes later, looking extremely hopeful. "Is it ready?"

"You bet," Jessica said. "Now, there's a tradition associated with the love potion. You have to drink it all in one gulp while holding your nose."

Peter wrinkled his nose. "Does it taste that horrible?"

"It's like cough syrup," Jessica said, handing him the bottle. "It has to taste bad, or it won't work."

Peter eyed the bottle suspiciously. "Are you *sure* this stuff works?"

Jessica threw up her hands. "Absolutely! Now hurry up, before it loses its power."

Peter took the top off the bottle and set it on the booth. Then, holding his nose with one hand, he lifted the bottle to his lips and drained it into his mouth. When he was done, he put the bottle down on the table. He seemed fine for a second or two—then he started fanning his mouth rapidly with his hand. "Hot!" he said, panting. "Water!"

Tamara handed him a few ice cubes. He put all three in his mouth at the same time.

Just when the effects of the hot sauces seemed to be dying down, Peter's face turned slightly pale. Then, as the Unicorns watched in fascination, he turned green. Jessica felt as if she were watching a science experiment.

"I don't feel very good," Peter said, wavering a little on his feet.

"I told you—love potion is powerful stuff," Jessica said, handing him the rest of her soda.

"Well, I guess this is all . . . worth it," Peter said, holding his stomach. He wandered off, sipping Jessica's root beer.

When he was out of earshot, everyone burst out laughing.

"My stomach hurts, too—from laughing!" Kimberly said.

"What did you put in there, anyway?" Tamara asked.

Jessica shrugged. "Beats me!"

"It was perfect, whatever it was. What a sucker!" Janet shook her head. "We should have sold him ten bottles!"

"I can't believe we sold all of the *Sixers* we printed," Elizabeth said as she got out of Mr. Bowman's car. "I thought we were going to be bringing a whole bunch back here to recycle."

"I think Amy deserves a lot of the credit," Mr. Bowman said, closing his door. "She's a terrific salesperson."

Mr. Bowman unlocked the front doors of the school, and they went inside. "I've been keeping the tickets in a very safe place," Mr. Bowman said. "And I apologize for that bad pun."

"What do you mean?" Amy asked.

"The tickets are in the school safe in Mr. Clark's

office. Since you two have tickets already, I assume you won't try to break in?"

"Not unless the tickets are closer than the seventh row," Amy said. "Just kidding."

"How do you want to work this drawing?" Elizabeth asked.

"Well, I have hundreds of raffle-ticket stubs that I'm going to put in this garbage can. Each one has a number as well as the person's name—in case they lose their stub," Mr. Bowman said. "I also did it that way to guarantee that each person had only one number. Writing down their names helped me keep track of who had already bought a ticket."

He opened a large cardboard box and shook the ticket stubs into the clean, empty trash can by his desk. "Elizabeth, will you do the honors? Amy, you're the witness to this procedure."

Amy nodded as Elizabeth stuck her hand into the trash can. She stirred the ticket stubs around for a minute, then closed her fingers on one. She couldn't help wishing that it would be Jessica's entry—and if not Jessica's, then Mary's. She pulled the ticket stub out and handed it to Mr. Bowman.

"Let's see . . ." He slipped his glasses on and stared at the stub. "Peter Burns."

"*Peter?*" Elizabeth said.

"Who were you expecting?" asked Mr. Bowman, looking at her strangely.

"Oh, no one," Elizabeth said. "It's just—I was

talking to him today, right before he bought his ticket, that's all."

"Peter really helped us out on this special edition—I like him," Mr. Bowman said. "Well, now that's settled, you girls can go home. Thank you very much for helping—and, needless to say, you are not to breathe a word of this to anyone, not even your goldfish. The announcement has to be a complete surprise tomorrow at the picnic."

"I won't say a word," Amy said. "Cross my heart. And I don't have any goldfish."

Elizabeth laughed. "Me neither."

As she left the building she couldn't help feeling pleased. Maybe Mary would have a chance to see Johnny Buck after all!

She wasn't sure who it would make happier— Peter or Mary.

That night, Mary was watching television by herself. Her parents had gone over to a friend's house, and she had nothing to do. That wasn't true, really—she could have gone over to Lila's with everyone else. But she didn't feel like celebrating their successful day at the carnival. She couldn't figure out why she was feeling so sad, either, which made it even worse.

The phone rang, and she reached to pick up the receiver from the coffee table. "Hello?"

"Mary, is that you?"

"Yeah. Hi, Tim."

"What's up? You sound weird," Tim said.

"I'm just sleepy," Mary said. "I've been watching a really boring movie."

"Oh. Why?" Tim asked.

"Because there's nothing else on," Mary said.

"Hey, did I tell you I bought a raffle ticket today?" Tim asked. "I mean, I think Johnny Buck stinks, but I thought maybe we could go together if you like him so much."

"That would be nice," Mary said. But she couldn't think of anyone she'd less like to see her favorite singer with. Tim would probably spend the entire time talking about how *he* really had a better voice than Johnny Buck.

"So, tomorrow you're going to get a ride to my house, right? And then my dad will take us from there," Tim said.

"Yeah, OK," Mary said. "Is there any way your father could pick me up on the way, though?"

"Oh, my dad said you live too far away," Tim explained.

Mary was starting to think that selfishness ran in the family. "What time should I be there?"

"How about eleven thirty? The picnic starts at noon," Tim said. "Listen, I gotta run. I'm going to get ice cream with the guys."

After Mary hung up with Tim, she lay back down on the couch. She shut off the TV with the remote and turned on the radio instead. If Tim were nice, she thought, he would have tried to cheer her up. He would have asked her if *she* wanted to go get ice cream. *Peter would have*, she thought, as an image of Peter walking her home flashed into her mind. He'd been nice to her when she didn't win concert tickets. He'd given her that magazine. And she wasn't even dating him—now she was supposed to be dating Tim, and all he did was talk about himself.

Peter was really nice to me, and I was a jerk in return. Mary stared at the ceiling. No wonder he had decided he wasn't interested in her anymore. She wouldn't like someone who treated her the way she had treated Peter.

Maybe if she just told him that she'd only ignored him because her friends told her to, he would understand. But she knew that wasn't a good excuse. In fact, she felt terrible for having listened to them and not to herself.

I have to at least try to tell him how I feel, she thought. She decided to talk to him at the picnic the next day. Even if she was supposedly Tim's date, she was sure he'd take off with his friends and play basketball. Then maybe she'd have a chance to tell Peter she was sorry.

Who ever would have thought I'd be more anxious to talk to Peter Burns than to find out who won the Johnny Buck tickets? she thought, smiling at the ceiling.

Eleven

"Come on, Elizabeth. You *have* to tell me," Jessica said at breakfast on Sunday morning. For what was probably going to be the last time for a month, Jessica, Elizabeth, and Steven had shared the cleaning chores—although there wasn't much to do, since Steven had scoured the house for tickets the day before

Elizabeth calmly spread some butter on a blueberry muffin. "I can't tell you anything. Mr. Bowman made me promise."

"But I can't stand waiting anymore. I didn't sleep at all last night," Jessica complained. She gave Elizabeth her most pitiful look.

"Sorry," Elizabeth said. "You'll find out in a couple of hours, along with everyone else."

Jessica tapped her fingers on the table. There

had to be a way to make Elizabeth tell. "You know, if I wanted to, I could easily find out who won," she said.

"Really? How?" Elizabeth asked.

"Well, you know I can read your mind, if I really want to," Jessica said.

"Jessica, that never worked," Elizabeth said.

"All right, if you say so," Jessica said. "But I just haven't been using all my powers. Come on, let's try. If you concentrate really hard on the person's name, I'll think of it."

Elizabeth shook her head. "It's not going to work."

"Just try it," Jessica pleaded. "Come on. We'll warm up first. Think of a color."

Elizabeth nodded.

"It's blue, isn't it?" Jessica guessed.

"Red," Elizabeth said.

"That's OK, we're still warming up. Think of a number," Jessica said. "I say you're thinking of . . . nine."

"Eleven," Elizabeth said, smiling.

Jessica could tell that Elizabeth was enjoying proving her wrong. "OK, enough practice. The person who won the raffle is . . . Tom McKay."

"No."

"I'll tell you what. Write it on your napkin. That way I'll have something to visualize," Jessica suggested.

"Jessica!" Elizabeth said, getting frustrated.

"Please? Pretty please? Here, I'll get you a pen."

Elizabeth sighed and quickly jotted down a name. "OK, one guess. I'm getting sick of this."

Jessica pretended to think for a moment, then shot her hand across the table and grabbed the napkin.

"Jessica Wakefield, I'm going to kill you!!!" Elizabeth screamed, chasing her sister out of the kitchen.

"I found them! I found them!" Steven was screaming as he danced into the living room.

Mr. Wakefield let out a loud sigh. "Thank goodness. Now maybe life will go back to seminormal around here."

"What do you mean, you found them?" Jessica demanded. It was no fair, Steven finding his tickets without her! First Peter won the raffle, and now this? "Where were they?"

"You're not going to believe this," Steven said. He pulled out a chair and sat down at the dining-room table. "They were in my geometry book—which was sitting right there in the middle of my desk this whole time!" He shook his head and helped himself to a blueberry muffin. "Can you believe it?"

Mr. Wakefield loudly cleared his throat. "No, I can't believe it. Are you telling me that this is the first time you've looked at your geometry book in over a *week*?"

Jessica grinned. Maybe Steven was going to the concert, but she had a feeling that was the end of the good news.

Steven swallowed hard. "Well . . . uh . . . we had some handouts and stuff," Steven said. "You know how it is."

"Not quite," Mr. Wakefield said. "I was under the impression that you used that book regularly for homework assignments. Isn't that true?"

"Well, yeah, but—I don't know." Steven looked up sheepishly. "I guess I've been pretty busy looking for those tickets this week."

"Well, in order to help you get caught up, I'd like you to stay close to home next week," Mr. Wakefield said solemnly.

"In other words, you're grounded," Jessica said, making no attempt to hide her glee.

Steven dropped the muffin on its way to his mouth. "But—Dad—the concert—"

"Relax. You can take Cathy to the concert Tuesday night," Mr. Wakefield said.

Steven looked triumphantly across the table at Jessica.

"Oh, shut up," she grumbled. Her last chance at going to the concert was blown. Even Steven being grounded didn't cheer her up. She was going to be stuck cleaning for a month. Her skin would wrinkle, her back would hurt. . . .

There were only two possibilities left. She

could try to impersonate Elizabeth the night of the concert. But that would mean she'd have to tie up Elizabeth, and she didn't want to do that. It wasn't Elizabeth's fault she was lucky.

Her last option was a personal appeal to Johnny Buck. "Dear Johnny," she thought. "Please let me come to the concert, or I'm going to have dishpan hands for the rest of my life."

Jessica kept glancing at the phone and drumming her fingers on the wall. The only way she'd persuaded Elizabeth not to murder her was by swearing she wouldn't tell anybody else who'd won the raffle. She'd kept the secret for a whole hour, and it was killing her. She didn't want to break her promise, but she was dying to call somebody. After everything that had happened with Mary and Peter, she couldn't believe he was the one who'd won.

Jessica went over to the bottom of the stairs. Steven and Elizabeth were in their rooms—they wouldn't hear her. Her parents had gone for a walk. It wouldn't hurt to tell just *one* person, would it?

"Lila, I have something big to tell you," Jessica said when Lila picked up the phone. "Really big."

"You're broke, and you need to borrow some money," Lila said. "I'm shocked."

"*No*," Jessica said in an exasperated tone. "It's about the raffle. I happen to know who won."

"What? How do you know?" Lila asked.

"A little bird told me," Jessica said. "A little bird named Elizabeth, who helped Mr. Bowman pick the winning ticket yesterday after the carnival."

"You actually got her to tell you?" Lila said.

"Yup," Jessica said. "You're not going to believe who won. But before I say anything, you have to promise to keep this a total secret."

"Is it you?" Lila asked excitedly. "Are you calling to ask me to go with you? Or—wait—it's me, isn't it?"

"Not even close," Jessica said. "Do you promise not to tell?"

"Of course I do," Lila said. "Now, who won?"

"It's Peter—Puppy Love Peter!"

"No way!" Lila said. "Are you serious? But— you know what that means." She laughed. "Mary should never have dumped him!"

"I know," Jessica said. "If she hadn't, she'd be going to see Johnny Buck. I mean, who cares who you go with—I was even willing to go with Steven, if he asked me."

"Maybe she could still get him to take her," Lila suggested.

Jessica giggled. "If he's still alive, after drinking that stuff I mixed up yesterday." Then she thought of something. If it really didn't matter who she went to the concert with . . . maybe she should try to get Peter to take her. He'd probably be glad to get *any* date, even if it was with the girl who'd made him drink a disgusting-tasting love potion. "Listen, Lila, I have to go. I'll meet you at the picnic, OK? And don't tell anyone!"

Jessica hung up the phone and grabbed the telephone book. But as she riffled through the pages looking for Peter's number, she started thinking about Mary, and how sad she'd seemed ever since losing at the ticket drawing. Mary was the person who really deserved to see Johnny Buck. And Mary was the one Peter liked.

With a sigh, Jessica called Mary's house instead of Peter's. Her father answered the phone. "Hi, Mr. Wallace, is Mary there?"

"No, I'm sorry, Jessica," Mr. Wallace said. "She's already left for the picnic."

"But—it doesn't start for almost an hour," Jessica said.

"Her mother was dropping her off at Tim's house, and they're leaving together from there," Mr. Wallace explained. "Should I give her a message?"

"No—I'll see her at the picnic," Jessica said. "Thanks!" After she had hung up the phone, she sat at the kitchen table, staring out the window. Well, it wasn't as if she hadn't *tried* to do the right thing. Anyway, Mary was dating Tim now—she probably wouldn't be interested in Peter even if he knew Johnny Buck personally.

She ran upstairs to change her clothes, taking the stairs two at a time. Maybe today wasn't going to be such a bad day after all!

Mary had been sitting in the living room, looking at magazines, for fifteen minutes before Tim came downstairs to greet her. "Hey," he said when he walked into the room. "Sorry—I woke up late."

"It's OK," Mary said, shrugging. She was still anxious to get to the picnic on time, though, just in case Peter didn't stick around long.

"It turns out my dad can't drive us after all," Tim said, tossing a basketball back and forth. "So we'll have to ride bikes."

"But—I don't have my bike," Mary said.

"It's OK, you can use my mom's," Tim said. "Come on."

They went outside to the garage, and Tim showed her which bike was hers. "Isn't Secca Lake kind of a long ride from here?" Mary said, glancing down at her new sundress as she got on the bike. The frame was too big for her—she could reach the pedals only if she stood up. "I could always ask my mother to come get us."

"No, it doesn't take that long," Tim said, taking off down the driveway. "Come on!"

Mary rode after him, straining to pick up some speed. But the bike was old and heavy and she had to stand the entire time. After riding for about ten minutes, she was exhausted. Tim was still about a hundred yards ahead of her, as if he couldn't bear to be seen riding with a girl.

All of a sudden there was a rumbling sound in the back tire. Mary looked down. It was completely flat.

"Tim! I have a flat tire!" she called ahead to him, but he didn't seem to hear. She stopped and got off the bike. That was when she saw it: There was black grease all over the side of her new sundress, from where it had been hitting the chain. She felt like crying.

"What's going on?" After riding ahead for a couple of minutes, Tim had finally circled back to Mary.

"Flat tire." Mary pointed to the rear tire.

"How did that happen?" Tim asked, sounding irritated.

"I don't know—the tube's probably old, like the rest of the bike," Mary said, feeling angry.

Tim shook his head. "My mom rides it all the time, and she's never had a problem. You must have run over something sharp."

"If she rides it all the time, maybe the tire's worn *out*," Mary said. "I didn't see anything sharp on the road."

"You must not have been paying attention," Tim said.

"If I wasn't, it's because I was trying to stay on

this bike, which is about six inches too big for me!" Mary complained.

"Well, you don't have to get all mad about it," Tim said. "It's not my fault you didn't watch where you were going."

Mary glared at him. If this was his idea of a date, then she had had enough. "Why don't you ride ahead. I'll have to walk. Is it OK if I lock the bike to that street sign over there? I don't want to push it the whole way."

"I guess so," Tim said. He started to ride off, then stopped and circled back. "Are you sure you want to walk? I could try to carry you on the handlebars."

"No, I'll walk," Mary said. "I'll meet you at the picnic."

"OK!" Tim sped off down the street.

"What a jerk," Mary grumbled as she locked the bike to the sign. The key was in the lock, so she could use it—at least *something* on the bike worked.

She was glad they'd made it far enough that she knew where she was going. Secca Lake was only about a half hour's walk away. Mary had all the energy she needed: She couldn't wait to get to the picnic. One reason was that she wanted to talk to Peter, to try to explain what an idiot she'd been. The other reason was that she was going to tell Tim she never wanted to see him again!

Twelve

By the time Mary got to Secca Lake, the picnic was already in full swing. A group of kids was playing volleyball, loud music was blaring, and hamburgers and chicken were cooking on the barbecue grills. A long table in the middle of everything was covered with food. Mary quickly scanned the crowd. She saw Tim playing volleyball. She was about to march over to him and tell him off when she spotted Peter at the food table. She almost hadn't seen him, because he was surrounded by girls!

Not just any girls, either—all of her friends were crowded around him. Jessica, Lila, Mandy, Tamara, and even Janet! *What's going on?* she thought. Had everyone suddenly realized what she had—that Peter was a great guy, even if he wasn't the coolest boy in school?

She headed over to the table. She didn't care if all her friends did want to talk to Peter. She was the one who had liked him first.

"Hey, Mary, you made it!" Tim called to her as she passed the volleyball game.

"No thanks to you!" she yelled back just as Tim dove for a shot.

He got up from the sand and gave her a stunned look. "Me? What did I do?"

"Nothing—that's the point!" Mary said. She heard some of his friends laughing as she kept walking. She hoped they were laughing at him and not her. As she approached the table, she could hear Jessica talking.

"So, I'm really sorry I gave you that bad love potion yesterday," Jessica was saying. "It wasn't until later that I realized I put a little of my dad's extra-hot barbecue sauce into the bottle by mistake. But the rest of the ingredients were one-hundred-percent love potion."

Peter didn't look convinced. *What love potion?* Mary wondered. She didn't know Peter had come by their booth. And what had Jessica given him?

"That's OK," Peter said. "As long as it works." He smiled.

"It's working now, isn't it?" Lila cooed. "I mean, when's the last time you were surrounded by so many pretty girls?"

"Uh . . . never?" Peter said, laughing.

"I told you our love potion was guaranteed," Janet said, giving Peter a big smile. "And now it's up to you. You could probably go out with any girl you wanted." She moved a little closer to him.

"Peter!" Mary said loudly. She stepped forward and grabbed his arm. "We need to talk."

"We do?" Peter looked nervous as she gently pulled him away from the table.

"Yes," Mary said. She led him away from the crowd and sat him down underneath a large tree. "There's something I want to get straight."

Peter just looked at her. He seemed too afraid to say anything.

Mary took a deep breath. "I'm sorry I acted like such a jerk toward you. I know you liked me, and I liked you, too—only my friends didn't think I should be nice to you. So I wasn't." She shook her head. "Everyone thought that I should go out with Tim instead—boy, were they wrong. He's the most conceited person I've ever met. Anyway, the point is, he's nowhere near as nice as you. And I just want to apologize for being mean, and tell you that I—well, I really like you."

"You do?" Peter's expression was one of total amazement. Then he grinned. "I'm not surprised. It's because of the love potion."

"The *love* potion?" Mary laughed. "There's no such thing, Peter. We just made it up!"

"Maybe you did, but it worked," Peter said.

"Did you see everyone talking to me over there?"

"Yeah . . . but . . . " Mary didn't know what to say. She couldn't explain that, either! "But all we did was make a recipe for pineapple punch and color it purple."

"Pineapple?" Peter shook his head. "More like tomato!"

"What are you talking about?" Mary asked.

"When I got to your booth, the potion was sold out, so Jessica made up a special batch for me," Peter said. "Do you think maybe that batch worked?"

"I think they were playing a practical joke on you," Mary said.

"Then how do you explain the fact that you're talking to me now—and telling me you like me and everything?" Peter asked.

"Because I had time to think about it," Mary said. "I don't like you because of some silly love potion."

"Really?" Peter asked.

"Really."

Peter relaxed. "That's a relief. If I had to keep drinking that stuff, I think my stomach would self-destruct in about a week."

Mary laughed. "Was it that horrible?"

"Worse," Peter said. "But you know, I was willing to try anything." He smiled at her.

"How come you didn't give up on me when I started hanging around with Tim?" Mary asked.

"I may not be the coolest guy at school, but I know a jerk when I see one!" Peter said. "I figured you'd realize that and dump him pretty quickly."

"So you don't think *I'm* a jerk for treating you the way I did?" Mary asked.

"No," Peter said. "Now Jessica, on the other hand . . ."

"May I have your attention—your attention, please," Mr. Bowman practically shouted over the small PA system he had borrowed from school for the picnic.

"Is he trying to destroy our hearing?" Janet complained. She stood on her tiptoes and looked around the crowd. "Do you see Peter anywhere?"

"He's over by the grill—with Mary," Jessica said. She glanced around the crowd. "Does it seem to you guys like there are about ten times more couples than usual here today?"

"Yes," Lila said. "I don't know what their problem is."

"It's weird," Jessica said. "It's almost like—"

They all turned and stared at each other.

"You don't think it was the love potion?" Jessica said.

"Maybe it was more powerful than we thought," Mandy said with a mysterious smile.

"Is everybody ready?" Mr. Bowman asked the crowd. "Before I announce the winner of the

Johnny Buck raffle, I want to introduce Mr. Clark, who's going to say a few words about yesterday's carnival." He moved away from the microphone, making room for Mr. Clark.

"Good afternoon!" Mr. Clark said, smiling broadly. "Congratulations are in order. Yesterday's carnival raised more money than *any* carnival in the past!"

A loud cheer went up from the crowd.

"I'm sure our booth made the most money," said Janet. "We'll win the award, and everyone will know we're the best at everything."

"What do you think it'll be?" Mandy asked.

"Money, of course," Lila told her.

"Or gift certificates from the mall," Jessica said.

"And, as promised, there's a special award this year for the group that raised the most money for charity," Mr. Clark said. "It is my pleasure to give this award to . . . the Unicorn Club!"

"Yeah!" Jessica yelled, following everyone up front to accept the award. She couldn't wait to see what it was.

"Congratulations," Mr. Clark said, handing Janet a wooden plaque. "You've really helped the community."

"A lousy *plaque*?" Lila muttered under her breath—only she was so close to the microphone that it picked up her voice and broadcast her comment to the crowd.

Everyone in the audience started laughing, and Lila's face turned red. "Ah, thank you very much," she said, turning her brightest smile on Mr. Clark.

They went back to their spot to wait for the raffle results. "Nice going, Lila," Mandy said. "Way to make us look bad."

"I think it's nice," Belinda said. "They didn't have to give us anything!"

"Belinda's right," Jessica agreed. "Although a cash bonus would have been nicer."

"All right! Drumroll, please!" Mr. Bowman cried. "The winner of the raffle for Johnny Buck concert tickets—and by the way, thanks to everybody who participated—is . . . Peter Burns!"

"Yeah, yeah," Jessica muttered, "we know."

Everyone applauded as Peter walked up to Mr. Bowman to get the tickets. They shook hands, and then Peter went back to Mary and handed her one ticket out of the envelope. She looked completely surprised—and very happy. Jessica was happy for her. She did deserve to see the concert, even if she *had* chosen the wrong time to decide she liked Peter.

Suddenly Peter began walking toward the Unicorns. *Oh, no. Now he's going to tell me off,* Jessica thought. *He knows about the love potion.* Then an even worse thought occurred to her. *No—now he knows why we were all being so nice to him, and he's going to tell us off for that! And then Elizabeth will know I told.*

"Why is he coming over here?" Lila wondered out loud.

"Maybe he'll give one of us the other ticket," Ellen said.

"I think he liked me better than any of you," Janet said as Peter approached them.

He walked past Tamara, Ellen, Mandy, Lila, and Janet—and stopped in front of Jessica. He held out the ticket to her. "Have a good time at the concert," he said.

"Are you serious?" Jessica shrieked. "Do you mean I can go with Mary?"

"Sure," Peter said, smiling. "After all, without that special, extra-strength love potion you brewed for me, Mary and I wouldn't be together now."

What a sucker, Jessica thought. But what an incredibly *nice* sucker! She threw her arms around Peter. "Thank you! Thank you! You've saved my life!"

"No problem," Peter said. "The truth is, I don't really like Johnny Buck very much. Don't tell Mary, but his voice gives me a headache. Well, I'd better get back to Mary before that *potion* wears off." Then he smiled at her.

Jessica was astonished—Peter had known all along! Even her little joke on him hadn't stopped him from being nice to her. *I guess we really were wrong about him,* Jessica thought as she watched him walk away.

"I can't believe it. After all this, I'm actually going to the concert!" Jessica screamed. She turned to flash a big smile at the rest of the Unicorns, who were sitting around Lila's bedroom after the carnival.

Ten angry faces looked back at her.

"I bet he won't even play that long," Janet said, frowning. "I mean, it's only Sweet Valley."

"I don't know why he picked you," Lila grumbled. "I'm the one who sent in all those entries. I should be going."

"I can't believe it," Jessica said for the ninth time. "After all that work and all that worrying, Peter Burns is the one who gives me a ticket." She shook her head.

Lila eyed her suspiciously. "Don't think we didn't know what you were up to, either," she said, rolling her eyes.

"What do you mean?" Jessica asked.

"We were onto you from day one," Lila said. "That day at the pool. Do you think we didn't notice you trying to butter us up so we'd invite you to the concert if we got tickets?"

"Me? Butter you up?" Jessica asked, trying to look innocent.

"Jessica, when's the last time you volunteered to

get me anything to drink?" Lila replied. Then she smiled. "Actually, it was kind of fun—especially when you almost got sick, watching that awful movie. Your face was green, even in the dark!" Lila laughed.

"Laugh all you want—*I'm* going to the concert," Jessica snapped.

Thirteen

"Whooooeeee!!" Jessica yelled as she danced around her room. "Johnny Buck, here we come!" It was Tuesday evening, and she and Mary were getting ready for the concert together.

Mary laughed. "I can't wait."

"By the way," Jessica said, standing still for a moment. "You won't tell Elizabeth all the stuff I just told you, will you?" she asked Mary. "She still doesn't know I didn't keep the secret about Peter winning the raffle."

"Didn't she wonder why everyone was hanging around him at the picnic?" Mary asked. She ran a brush through her long hair.

"I guess she got there after you did, so he was off with you by then," Jessica said.

"Don't worry, I won't say anything," Mary said.

"I don't know if I'll even tell Peter. I kind of like the idea of him not knowing what it was that made everyone like him that day—although he must have already guessed."

"Hey, are you guys almost ready?" Elizabeth came into Jessica's room, followed by Amy.

"I think so," Mary said. "Only, I'm so nervous and excited I almost poked my eye out with Jessica's eye pencil."

"You look great," Amy said. "I love your outfit."

"Thanks," Mary said.

"This is pretty amazing, isn't it? We're all going, you, me, and Steven," Elizabeth commented.

"Practically a miracle," Jessica said. "Thanks to Peter."

"He's really sweet, isn't he?" Mary said, leaning against the doorway.

"Definitely," Jessica said, checking her reflection in the mirror one last time. "Whatever you do, Mary, don't dump him, OK? He's a pretty great guy."

Mary just shook her head and laughed.

"Dad," Steven said, shaking his head. "Dad, I am *not* showing up at the concert with *them*."

"Come on, it'll be fine," Mr. Wakefield said. "Now, we'd better get going, so we can pick up Cathy."

Steven groaned and pretended to bang his head against the wall. "Why me? Stuck in a car with four shrieking girls—Dad, this is supposed to be a date, not a car pool to daycare."

"Cathy will be glad to have us. Otherwise she'd be stuck with *you*," Jessica declared. "Anyway, it's not like we're sitting together."

"Come on, troops, let's go," Mr. Wakefield urged. They filed out the door to the garage and, one by one, climbed into the car. "Now, before we go, I just want to ask one thing," Mr. Wakefield said. "Does everyone have their tickets?"

"Wait!" Steven cried.

Jessica laughed as the door flew open, and Steven jumped out and ran back into the house. He returned a minute later, clutching the tickets firmly in his hand.

"Where were they?" Jessica teased. "In your science book?"

"Don't be ridiculous," he said snidely. "Actually, in my Spanish book."

"If you guys don't stop talking about that concert, I'm going to scream," Lila said at lunch on Thursday. "I already know how great he looked, and how he went around the audience and stopped in front of your row and looked right at you."

Jessica sighed, indulging herself in the memory of Johnny Buck. Since the concert two nights before, she hadn't been able to think about anything—or anyone—else.

"Sorry," Mary said. "It's just that I still can't stop thinking about it." She shook some salt onto her french fries.

"Well, Johnny Buck's not the only musician around," Lila said. "Can't we at least talk about somebody else?"

"That reminds me—Melody Powers has a new video premiering soon," Mandy said.

"That's right—RockTV announced they would show it next week," Janet said, setting down her glass of water. "I'm psyched. Her videos are the best. Better than Johnny Buck's."

"We should watch it together," Tamara said.

"We'll watch it at my house," Lila announced. "Your TVs are all so *tiny*."

Jessica rolled her eyes. Sure, Lila had a big-screen TV and a living room the size of a football stadium, but she didn't need to brag about it all the time.

"I'll tell Daddy we want to make a pizza party out of it," Lila continued.

"Cool," Mandy said. "Have you guys seen that new show, where they put on local bands' videos?"

"Yeah. I'd do anything to get on that show—the winner gets to meet that incredibly gorgeous vee-jay," Ellen said.

"No problem," Jessica said with a shrug. "All we have to do is make our own video—and win!"

Everyone started laughing.
"Dream on, Jessica," Lila said.

What would happen if the Unicorns really did enter a video on RockTV? Find out in Sweet Valley Twins No: 73, LILA'S MUSIC VIDEO.

SWEET VALLEY TWINS

Don't miss the extra-long special editions of this
top-selling teenage series starring identical twins Jessica
and Elizabeth Wakefield and all their friends.

SUPER EDITIONS

> The Class Trip
> The Unicorns Go Hawaiian

SUPERCHILLERS

> The Ghost In the Graveyard
> The Carnival Ghost
> The Ghost In The Bell Tower